DOC SAVAGE'S AMAZING CREW

William Harper Littlejohn, the bespectacled scientist who was the world's greatest living expert on geology and archaeology.

Colonel John Renwick, "Renny," his favorite sport was pounding his massive fists through heavy, paneled doors.

Lieutenant Colonel Andrew Blodgett Mayfair, "Monk," only a few inches over five feet tall, and yet over 260 pounds. His brutish exterior concealed the mind of a great scientist.

Major Thomas J. Roberts, "Long Tom," was the physical weakling of the crowd, but a genius at electricity.

Brigadier General Theodore Marley Brooks, slender and waspy, he was never without his ominous, black sword cane.

WITH THEIR LEADER, THEY WOULD GO ANYWHERE, FIGHT ANYONE, DARE EVERYTHING—SEEKING EXCITEMENT AND PERILOUS ADVENTURE!

THE
FANTASTIC
ISLAND

A DOC SAVAGE ADVENTURE

BY KENNETH ROBESON

BANTAM BOOKS · TORONTO · NEW YORK · LONDON

THE FANTASTIC ISLAND
*A Bantam Book / published by arrangement with
The Condé Nast Publications Inc.*

PRINTING HISTORY

Originally published in DOC SAVAGE *Magazine December 1935*
Bantam edition / December 1966

2nd printing .. December 1966	5th printing .... July 1969
3rd printing .... July 1967	6th printing .. November 1969
4th printing ...... April 1968	7th printing .... July 1976

ISBN 0-553-10125-0

Published simultaneously in the United States and Canada

*Bantam Books are published by Bantam Books, Inc. Its trade-
mark, consisting of the words "Bantam Books" and the por-
trayal of a bantam, is registered in the United States Patent
Office and in other countries. Marca Registrada. Bantam
Books, Inc., 666 Fifth Avenue, New York, New York 10019.*

PRINTED IN THE UNITED STATES OF AMERICA

THE FANTASTIC ISLAND

Chapter I

SHIPWRECKS TO ORDER

THE disappearance of William Harper Littlejohn attracted no public attention whatever. The reason for this was simple. The public never learned about it.

William Harper Littlejohn was a very famous man. It was impossible that, if ten average men on the street should be stopped and asked who William Harper Littlejohn was, they would not have had the slightest idea; but, in his field, William Harper Littlejohn was tops. His field was archæology and geology. Wherever men are interested in such things, he was known.

William Harper Littlejohn's disappearance was simple. He had chartered a ship and was taking an archæological expedition to the Galapagos Islands, below the equator in the Pacific Ocean. The Galapagos are said to be the world's strangest islands. William Harper Littlejohn simply disappeared. The ship vanished also. The whole expedition, too.

It could not have been that their radio merely failed. There were three radio transmitters on the expedition ship. No, there was some other reason. It was strange.

Just how strange it was, no one had any idea at the beginning of the thing.

William Harper Littlejohn happened to be one of the five men associated with that remarkable man of mystery, Doc Savage. Word of his disappearance reached Doc Savage at his New York headquarters. Doc Savage acted promptly.

Two of Doc Savage's aids—he had five of them altogether—were on a vacation cruise in the yacht *Seven Seas*, which chanced to be off the coast of Panama, in the Pacific. Aboard the yacht also was Patricia Savage, a remarkable young woman, whose relationship to Doc Savage was that of cousin. Pat had gone along for the trip, she claimed; but

1

it was to be suspected that she was looking for excitement.

If she was looking for excitement, she was certainly destined to find it.

Doc Savage, man of bronze, individual of mystery, mental wizard and physical marvel—to quote the newspapers—sent a radiogram to the yacht *Seven Seas* headed for the Galapagos to look for William Harper Littlejohn, who was better known as "Johnny," and his expedition.

The *Seven Seas* was now about to slam headlong into more trouble than those aboard would ever have believed possible.

THE *Seven Seas* was riding a radio beam radiated, by special courtesy on the part of the powerful United States Naval radio station, from the Panama Canal Zone. This beam simplified navigation, and they were riding it straight for the Galapagos.

Brigadier General Theodore Marley Brooks stood on the dripping deck of the *Seven Seas* and stared into an immensity of black sky and blacker water. Occasionally he scowled anxiously upward at the radio rigging. Water slapped and phosphoresced around the bow.

Right now, the yacht was rolling in a huge ground swell, rolling alarmingly. Rivets strained and bulkheads creaked. There was at least half a gale blowing, and it made noises in the rigging like the sighs of dying men.

Brigadier General Theodore Marley Brooks was commonly called "Ham," a name which he did not like. He now frowned darkly and made his way to the pitching bridge.

"This is dangerous," he snapped. "We may run onto a reef any minute."

"Don't I know it?" a surprisingly childlike voice retorted from the semidarkness of the bridge. "This ground swell is bad—mighty bad. When it piles up like this, it means the water is getting shallow."

Ham snapped, "But I thought you said——"

"Something screwy," piped the childlike voice. "According to our log, we're supposed to have more than a hundred miles between us and the nearest land."

A young woman joined them on the bridge. She was a very striking young woman to look at, having not only a lovely face, but hair of a very unusual bronze color and eyes which actually looked golden. She was Patricia Savage, who loved excitement.

"I wish you'd ask your old ocean to behave," she requested, cheerfully. "I've been thrown out of my bunk three times in the last fifteen minutes. I gave it up."

"Something is wrong, Pat," Ham told her. "We're getting into a big ground swell. That means we are near land, or at least in shoal water. And that is very much impossible."

Pat walked over to the second man on the bridge.

"Just what is the trouble, Monk?" she asked.

The man addressed as "Monk" sat in the shadows, hunched like a bulky Buddha over an audio-frequency amplifier. His thick hands indicated the apparatus containing vacuum tubes for increasing the voltage and power of radio beacon signals.

"These direction-finding doodads have gone plain haywire," he insisted in that small squeaky voice.

Ham joined them and listened to the signal pulsations coming from the loudspeaker. He said, "The beat frequency is sounding just as it should. We are certainly not off the course as broadcast to us from the government radio beacon in the Canal Zone."

"We're right in the beam, all right," Monk grunted. "The A wave is jammed with the N waves so you don't hear any dots—just a blur of dashes. We can't be off our course, *but we must be.*"

"Impossible!" snapped Ham. "Our goniometer, with its new type amplifier developed by Doc Savage himself, insures that the direction finder couldn't go wrong. And the United States government station is transmitting the beam to us."

THE word exchange had the rather unexpected effect of throwing Monk into what looked like a very violent rage.

"You tellin' me, you courtroom fop?" Monk growled belligerently at Ham.

"Don't get tough with me, you missing link," Ham snapped. "I'll make shark bait out of you!"

Monk pushed back from the radio apparatus and squared off threateningly before Ham.

"Who says I'm wrong?" he demanded in a voice no longer mouselike.

"I did, you ape," Ham snapped.

"You're a liar besides bein' a shyster lawyer," Monk bellowed. "I'm right, and you know darned well that I'm right!"

Pat said dryly, "I wonder if you know what you're quarreling over."

The two men pretended not to hear. Ham and Monk seemed always on the point of taking each other apart violently. The mildest word from one was likely to set the other off in a rage; but it was only on rare occasions that their enmity extended beyond the talking stage.

Patricia Savage cast an idle glance around the horizon. She started violently.

"Look!" she cried. "Ahead there, a bit to port. Green and red lights!"

"Huh?" Monk jerked around. "Channel lights that sounds like."

Ham stared intently, forgot himself and his feud with Monk. "Channel lights they are, but they were not there a minute ago."

Monk's small eyes blinked rapidly. "It ain't possible."

"Some mistake," Ham muttered. "No lights are indicated on the chart."

Pat pointed at them and said, "There they are," with inescapable feminine logic.

Ham and Monk crowded forward for another inspection of the charts. They offered a strange contrast in appearance, these two men. Ham was meticulously attired in a blue marine uniform, a blue cap with its insignia in gold set jauntily on his head. He carried a slender black cane. He was handsome, lithe, and wore his clothes like a fashion plate.

Monk, on the contrary, wore a not too white pair of duck pants, wrinkled across the thighs and bagged at the knees. An enormous green-and-white-striped undershirt fitted around his barrel chest like a circus tent slipped on over an elephant. Rusty hair stuck out on his bulletlike head like mashed bristles on a wire brush. The hair grew low down on his forehead, half burying his ears, almost meeting his scrubby eyebrows. His homely face was mostly mouth and flat nose. His body was nearly as wide as it was long and his fists hung down almost to his knees. In fact, he did not look like a man. He resembled an amiable ape.

It was a mistake to judge either of these two by appearances. Ham was no fop. He was one of the most astute lawyers Harvard had ever turned out. And Monk, as Lieutenant Colonel Andrew Blodgett Mayfair, was recognized as one of the greatest, living, industrial chemists.

The greatest claim to distinction of these two men, however, was that they were members of Doc Savage's group of five remarkable aids. That alone made them unusual, for each of the bronze man's five aids was a master of some particular profession.

Pat went over now and disconnected the robot control which had been steering the ship.

"Shall I hold to the channel lights?" she asked, swinging the wheel slightly over.

"I don't like this," Ham said, uneasily. "There should be no harbor at all near us, least of all a lighted harbor, even a lighted channel. But there is nothing else to do."

"Why not?" Monk demanded. "We don't have to go in that channel, do we?—if there is a channel."

Ham snapped, "It's worth investigating. That is what I mean."

It looked as if their perpetual quarrel were going to break out again.

Pat solved the problem by turning the *Seven Seas* toward the channel markers.

THE yacht was caught in a choppy cross-current now, and the wind was rising. It no longer sighed like men at death's door. It wailed and howled.

Ham went to the end of the bridge and clung to the railing to keep from being pitched off the violently tilting craft into the boil of black water around them. In spite of the wind, the night was oppressive, muggy, with a faint sulphurous smell. Suddenly a flickering glow, as of sheet lightning, sprang into life, tinging the low-hanging clouds.

Ham made a mistake. He dismissed it at first as ordinary lightning. Then he saw that there was something different about these luminous flashes. They were weird, unearthly. They stained the low-hanging clouds a bloody red.

Ham heard a rasped breath behind him and was startled into whirling. It was Monk.

"Red lightnin'," Monk uttered, hanging on against the fetid, sulphurous wind at the deck tip. "That's funny-lookin', ain't it?"

Again the gory light mushroomed out under the clouds. It was more sustained, brighter this time, and it showed them things. Off to one side bulked a shore line; but this did not strike them with terror. Pat called attention to the thing that did.

"Look!" she screamed. "Look! All around us!"

"Hard alee!" Monk squalled. "Engines reversed!"

The fantastic red light went out.

"Did you see?" Ham gasped in the silence that followed. "There must be two dozen ships, big and little, wrecked all around us."

"And the devil only knows where we are," Monk gulped. "I'm gonna back this boat, turn around, get outta here an' wait for daylight."

"A whole graveyard of wrecked ships," Pat gasped. "Red lightning that smells of sulphur!"

Pat's voice sounded, it seemed, rather cheerful.

"You always did like trouble, didn't you?" Monk grunted at her.

"And mystery," Pat added. "I eat it up."

There must have been a tide that carried the *Seven Seas* to one side, or something. They were in reverse, exactly re-tracing the course they had been sailing, when it happened.

A curling wave lifted the bow of the *Seven Seas* high in the water and hurled it down. The yacht shuddered with a wrenching shock that knocked Monk and Ham sprawling on the wet deck. There was a nightmare of grinding and scrapings as steel plates were wrenched from the hull by jagged coral.

Caught fast on the submerged reef, the craft did not rise with the next wave. She heeled half over instead, with a groaning of tortured steel; and the wave washed in an avalanche of water over the deck.

Ham and Monk were battered against the anchor winch. They staggered up, half drowned, to claw their way toward the bridge.

"Aid Pat, if she needs it," Monk bellowed. "Me, I'm goin' for Habeas Corpus!"

Habeas Corpus was Monk's cherished pet pig. He never went anywhere without the animal, much to Ham's disgust and frequent infuriation.

A streak of light, blue-white, darted from the *Seven Sea's* bridge, knifed across the rock-fanged water.

"Turn that searchlight off," Ham shouted to Pat, as he went down again under a drenching cross-wave.

"It'll help us see to swim ashore," Pat protested.

"It'll draw sharks," Ham snapped, as he caught the life preserver Pat threw him.

"So you're afraid of sharks," Pat said.

But she switched off the searchlight and joined Ham at the submerged rail. Monk appeared on deck an instant later with the squealing, kicking armful of razorback hog that was Habeas Corpus.

Habeas Corpus had a snout like a wood-rasp, flopping coal-scuttle ears, long ungainly legs. The special life preserver which Monk had previously fashioned for Habeas did not improve his appearance. It added to his buoyancy, however. Monk jumped into the water with the wet pig.

"That hog'll draw sharks," Ham yelled.

"Habeas, he fight sharks!" Monk roared back. "Come on!"

PAT and Ham went overboard, Ham still holding tightly to his slim black cane which was almost as much a part of him as his shirt. The cane was in reality a formidable weapon —a sword cane. Its innocent-appearing exterior sheathed a length of gleaming steel, the point of which had been impregnated with a chemical capable of producing almost instant unconsciousness.

Under the red lightning glare, surf on all sides broke against hidden reefs, churning the water to a bloody froth. But Pat and Ham came through the barrage of wave-lashed rocks and reeled, half drowned and gasping, onto a mangrove-studded beach. Monk swashed ashore close behind them, holding the squirming Habeas Corpus under an arm with difficulty.

"That hog'll kick a rib out for you some day," Ham warned, breathing hard.

"Lay off Habeas Corpus," Monk gasped, "or I'll be kickin' out some ribs on my own account."

The red luminance bloomed again against the clouds. It crawled and writhed, disappeared, and blanketed out again like a bloody mist floating in air.

"What is it?" Pat demanded, shivering in spite of the sultry night.

"Nothing supernatural," Ham explained. "You notice the color on the clouds does not seep through from above. The light is reflected from underneath——"

"There's an active volcano somewhere on the island," Monk summed up.

Pat pressed water out of her drenched hair. "Do you suppose here's where Johnny is?"

"We'll have to find out," Ham said, grimly.

"One thing I'd like to clear myself on," Pat said earnestly. "The shipwreck. I was holding dead in the middle of the channel when it happened."

"Yeah," Monk agreed, "it wasn't your fault."

"This shipwreck was *arranged*," Ham said, ominously.

"Some one on this island set those lights so we'd run slam on the reef, you mean?" Monk muttered.

Ham said soberly, "Some one drew us a hundred miles off our course and wrecked us. We're up against something really sinister."

"Kinda wish Doc was here," Monk announced.

The next moment he was wishing it even more violently.

Attracted perhaps by the blue-white searchlight beam which had lanced out from the *Seven Seas* a moment after she had gone on the rocks, shadowy man-figures loosened from the darkly entwined mangrove thicket and bore down upon the castaways, brandishing short clubs and shrieking a harsh unintelligible gibberish.

Chapter II

ISLAND OF HORROR

THE dimly seen attackers, twenty or more, rushed out of the mangroves in a solid wave. Ham and Monk thrust Pat behind, then met the attack—Ham with his sword cane, Monk with his granite-knuckled fists.

Ham dropped two of the assailants with deft thrusts of the sword cane. He was careful not to allow the valuable cane, tipped with the unconsciousness-producing chemical, to be struck; in fact, Ham was more regardful of the cane than of himself.

Unexpectedly, there was an ugly-sounding whack, and Ham staggered back groggily from a club which had bludgeoned past his guard. Dazedly, he saw the club lift again. But it did not descend. Not with any weight behind it. There was a rap of knuckles against a jaw as Monk's long arm jabbed out and knocked the club-swinger off his feet.

Ham recovered his balance and got his deadly sword cane into use again.

"Let's charge 'em," Monk squawled.

"Righto," Ham agreed. "We'll try to break through into the mangroves!"

Side by side, they advanced into a rain of clubs—Monk's pummeling fists working like locomotive driving rods, Ham's sword cane darting in and out like an aroused snake. Pat, pressing forward behind them, scooped up rocks from the beach and threw them as fast as she could. Even Habeas Corpus did his part, squealing and grunting and gouging his sharp tusks into every foot and ankle that came within reach of his wood-rasp snout.

The varied strategy was too much for the attackers. They thought Ham's sword cane was dealing out death, and they broke suddenly, with hideous yells, to go crashing away and disappear in the black recesses of the mangrove sink.

Monk picked up Habeas Corpus and swung him lustily by the long ears, much to the pig's squealing delight. Monk grinned, and the action lighted up his unbelievably homely face, making it very pleasant to look at.

There was a little light now from the stars. Ham was making a quick examination of the anæsthetized victims of his sword cane.

They were of different races and colors—and all wore loin cloths. Their necks were encircled with copper-studded collars made, seemingly, out of lizard hide.

A great blast of noise riveted Ham's attention. It was only Monk laughing.

"What's the matter, you hairy ape?" Ham demanded, suspiciously.

"I was thinkin' how you'd look in the costume of the country—a loin cloth and a dog collar."

Ham bristled and gripped his sword cane tighter. "You wide-mouthed macaw——" he began.

Pat silenced him with tight-lipped words. "If you want more fighting, save your strength," she said. "They're coming back."

A LOUD *plud* sounded in the wet sand near Ham's feet. In a second the air was filled with heavy missiles. Habeas Corpus squealed.

"They're heaving rocks!" Ham shouted.

"They can throw more rocks than we can," Monk growled. "Let's get outta here."

Monk tucked one of the short, thick clubs under his arm, grabbed up Habeas Corpus by the ears, and lunged into the shadowed thicket. Pat and Ham followed closely.

Pressing through the mangrove sink, they came out upon a height of land that was nothing, if not weird. Volcanic rock, black lava sharp as broken glass, swallowed them up in a welter of fantastically shaped hills and gullies. Much of the razor-edged glass was in tilted sheets which were prone to slip and shatter under the weight of a footfall. Giant cactuses rooted in the crevices and dangled their spiny pads overhead, like hooded cobras ready to strike.

They lost all sounds of pursuit.

The low-raking clouds lifted and the three pressed on under the pale white light of equatorial stars.

"I hope we get somewhere quick," Pat said, appalled.

"They speak of the Galapagos archipelago as the 'world's end,' " Ham remarked.

"They don't miss it much," Monk grumbled. "How we're goin' to find Johnny in this volcanic scrap heap, I dunno."

"Did either of you get the impression," Pat asked suddenly, "that our League-of-Nations attackers were being careful not to kill us?"

"Yeah," Monk admitted. "Even those rocks were not thrown too hard."

"They wanted us alive, I guess," Ham supplied.

"My guess, too. But why?"

"That's anybody's guess."

"We could sure use Doc Savage about now."

Climbing higher up the glassy slope, they passed through a belt of cold volcanic pits and cones, where, ages before, the molten rock had bubbled like mush and cooled in scabrous pockmarks.

They came out on a wide plateau where nothing grew, not even the cobra-head cactus, and where the pits were smaller, clogged with earth and so close together that it was necessary to skirt the region to make any forward progress.

Monk stopped suddenly.

"These pits are all in geometric order," he declared. "They're not volcanic pits like the ones below. They're man-made."

Ham stared. On the plain, the glassy rock had given way to a kind of reddish clay, or hard-packed volcanic ash.

"Right," he clipped. "The pits are crumbling away now and mostly buried under loose earth. Hard to tell, but they must have been laid out originally with the regularity of cells in a honeycomb."

As they continued on, the honeycomb pattern became more apparent as the pits were revealed in a less crumbling condition.

"These were dug later," Ham observed.

"Yeah," Monk agreed. "The farther we go, the fresher the pits look."

"But what are they for?" Pat wondered. "Say, this all gets queerer and queerer. What's it all about?"

"LISTEN," Ham said, tensely.

Wafted on the miasmatic breeze came sharp, cracking sounds. There was unearthliness about the sounds, as though they sprang from the air of their own volition.

"What is it?" Pat asked uneasily.

"No animal ever made a sound like that," Monk blurted.

Suddenly through and above the cracking sounds, came a long-drawn wail which quavered up and down the scale in agony so appalling that a trickle of icy water seemed to be loosened on the back of each of the three listeners.

Pat gasped: "I never heard anything like it. Horrible!"

"A dying animal of some kind," Ham said.

"Dying man!" Monk corrected, grimly.

"Come on," Ham said, gripping his sword cane.

As they pressed forward, the pits in the rocklike ash actually became as sharply delineated as the cells in a honeycomb. A giant honeycomb. These pits were about ten feet in diameter, and some ten feet where they were not filled with loose earth. The mysterious cracking noises sounded louder.

"Ahead there," Ham rapped under his breath. "Look!"

"Shadows!" Pat gasped. "Like men moving!"

The three worked closer, holding to the concealment of the fringing thicket. White-pointed thorns tore at them, viciously shredding their clothes and piercing flesh. But they succeeded in approaching opposite the place where the shadows moved, and from where the cracking, cutting noises issued. Here the plain stretched on, but the advancing line of pits came to an end.

They crouched down, watching. Stars dripped pale light. And suddenly a close, bulking mountain disgorged a red glare into the sky. Bathed in the baleful light of volcanic fires, huge-muscled men could be seen moving ceaselessly up and down at the edge of the honeycombed ground. The men were clothed as those others had been—in loin cloths and leather collars. They carried long whips, which they swung over their heads and cracked down into the row of pits.

Hideous groans and jabberings issued from the unseen depths of the pits. The whip-crackers, their half-naked bodies in the red volcanic glare sleek with glistening sweat, looked like satanic apparitions come to earth.

"Back on the yacht I said maybe we were headed for hell," Monk muttered. "Now, I know it!"

"The cracking noises we heard were from the whips," Ham observed.

"What's in the pits, I wonder?" Pat asked, in a hushed tone.

Monk was already edging forward, crawling on his stomach.

"Hold Habeas Corpus," he whispered back. "I'll find out."

"Blast your hog," Ham complained, but he held the pig.

As he muscled to a position where he could look down into

the pits, Monk gasped with grim surprise. In every one of the circular holes, as far as he could see down the long line, stakes were driven, and to the stakes were attached chains, and to the end of the chains were fastened men.

There was one man with a shovel in each pit, digging. The diggers wore loin cloths only, lacking the lizard-leather collars worn by the whip-cracking overseers. These collars Monk correctly assumed to be emblems of authority.

Each of the pit-men was digging a hole of a circumference allowed by the length of his chain. The holes, extending across the plain in a straight line, were of uniform width—about ten feet.

Under the lash of the whips, in the hellish red volcano glare, the chained men were actually digging their way to death.

SUDDENLY, from behind Monk, sounded a fast thudding on the hardpacked ground. Something thrust hard against his back as he swerved around. A shrill squeal sounded.

Monk clamped his huge hands over Habeas Corpus's snout to smother the affectionate squeals of the pig which had burst away from Ham and had run straight to Monk.

He throttled the squeals. But the damage was already done. Whip-cracking overseers jabbered sharply at each other and clumped forward to investigate the disturbance.

Monk's squat bulk reared upward. Brandishing his stout club, he lunged forward to meet the attack of the nearest man. But before Monk could close in, a deadly *swish* sounded. Monk's enemy was still six or eight paces away, but Monk felt his knees gripped as though by iron hands, jerked tightly together and pulled out from under him. He fell, striking the ground with stunning force.

Monk knew what had thrown him, and his hands raked down to jerk away the lead-tipped thong which had whipped out of the night murk and entwined his legs. Before he could free himself, his assailant was standing over him, the weighted whip handle raised high to crash against Monk's head.

Ham's sword cane slithered in that instant, dropped the overseer, and saved Monk from the blow. But another whip swished out of the night, wrapped around Ham's legs and hurled him to the ground on top of Monk.

Clubs battered them both to unconsciousness before they could claw free from the knee-binding thongs.

WHEN they came to, a few minutes later, they found

themselves bound and lying on the ground at the edge of the line of pits. Ham focused his groggy glance at the nearest pit worker. The man had sunk his hole about five feet down, so that his face was practically on ground level. That pain-racked face was almost within hand's reach of Ham.

Ham started violently. In a red volcanic flare he had recognized the man as being one of the members of Johnny's expedition.

"Tony!" Ham whispered hoarsely.

A shudder went over the man as his crazed eyes turned to Ham's. His lips widened in startled recognition. He said nothing, but kept on digging.

Ham shot a quick glance around, saw that the nearest overseer was intently engaged in a bullying cross-examination of Pat. Ham squirmed close to the edge of the hole, so that his lips were almost at the digger's ear.

"Where's the rest of the ship's crew—and Johnny?" he whispered.

"Crew's in the pits, diggin'," the man answered in a kind of wrenching sob.

"Where's Johnny? Is he alive?" Ham hung on the answer fearfully.

"Alive; but he won't be long."

"Where is he?"

"A big guy with a black beard took him away. I don't know where. I only know they're gonna kill Johnny. They're gonna kill all of us!" The man's voice rose to hysterical rasp.

"Don't talk so loud," Ham cautioned, fiercely. "What have we got into here? Tell me what you know. Quick! While we've got the chance."

"I can't tell you—but I can——" Then the man's voice rose in a choking shriek, out of all control now. It was an insane shriek.

Plainly, the fellow had broken under the tortures he had endured.

WHATEVER it was he meant to tell, or not to tell, Ham, remained forever untold. The overseer rushed forward, mouthing unintelligible curses. His arm reared up, and down. The leaded whip handle struck with gruesome thump against the crazed man's head. It was a blow heavy enough to have dropped anything alive. But the man in the pit was not exactly alive now. He was a raving madman, mercifully removed from all consciousness of pain. His whitish eyes rolled madly. Crimson foam bubbled from his lips.

The leaded whip handle descended again. This time the man slumped, a slack weight in the pit. He was dead before his body hit the bottom.

The overseer—he was some unidentifiable Asiatic type— bawled orders in harsh gibberish. Two guards shoved forward. One was a giant brown-skinned man; the other a paunchy Caucasian of indeterminate race. The brown man bent and commenced ripping the thongs from Ham's hands and feet. The other guard jumped heavily down, unlocked the iron cuff from the dead man's leg, and heaved the limp body out of the pit.

The guard on top grunted, and pushed Ham roughly over the edge. Ham fell sprawling. The guard in the pit was ready for him. He jangled the chain against the stake, grabbed Ham by the foot and slapped on the iron cuff, warm from the dead man's leg.

He picked up the dead man's shovel, thrust it into Ham's hands. The overseer above cracked down with the whip. A thick welt bloomed on Ham's cheek. He started digging.

Overseers herded Monk a short distance down the line of horror holes, and put him similarly to work.

Chapter III

PRISONERS OF THE PITS

PAT experienced a somewhat different fate from that of the two men. She was consigned to one of the pits; but, though she was chained to the stake, she was not whipped, nor was she compelled to dig.

She was greatly relieved at this concession to her womanhood until, cutting through the harsh medley of groans, whip-cracks and guttural cries, she heard the close voices of two guards conversing in English.

"Make her dig."

"No. The count will surely order her to be brought to the palace. He will not want her worn out from digging."

"But she could well stand a little bit of whipping——"

"No," the other protested. "In this case, the count will prefer to do his own whipping."

"Maybe you're right," the overseer growled, and moved away down the line of pits.

The other guard bent close over the edge of the hole. Pat shrank back. All at once, the pulse throbbed violently in her wrists and in her blue eyes sprang a look of desperate hope. She was recognizing this guard. He was another member of the expedition that had disappeared with Johnny.

"Aren't you——" she started to suggest.

"Al Fredrickton, first mate," he supplied.

"But you—that whip!"

"I have to whip to keep from being whipped," he whispered, savagely. "I'm on top to-day. To-morrow they may yank the collar off my neck and pitch me in a hole. I'm just as much a prisoner as these poor devils digging."

"But what is it all about?" Pat questioned.

"I don't know any more about it than you do. I only know that men dig and die."

"Dig and die!" she echoed, starkly. "What about Johnny?"

"He was taken to the palace. He may be alive. Listen: 33 Redbeach Road, Long Island. Can you remember that?"

"33 Redbeach Road—I've got it."

"Boris Ramadanoff, at that address."

"I've got it. What about it?"

The man's breath came faster. "You're our only hope," he rasped. "They'll take you to the palace. Try to contact Johnny. Tell him the name and address. There's a powerful short-wave radio sending set at the palace. Johnny must get a message to Doc Savage. Tell Doc Savage to contact Boris Ramadanoff."

"Yes, but what good will that do?"

"Ramadanoff can tell Doc Savage all he needs to know to effect our rescue. Ramadanoff is the brother of the big shot here on the island. They quarreled, the two brothers. And Boris left for New York."

"How did you find out all this?"

"After our ship followed in the false harbor lights and was wrecked, we were taken prisoners. The steward and I were retained to work in the palace kitchen. The steward heard the brothers quarreling. He learned Boris's new address and passed it on to me."

"Where is the steward?" Pat asked.

"Dead!" said the man. "They suspected he knew something. They killed him."

Pat shuddered. "Life isn't worth much here, is it?"

SOMETHING happened the next moment to demonstrate anew the fiendish ruthlessness of the sinister genius in control of this island.

A drumming beat sounded against the ground and a huge horse, ridden hard, snorted to a stiff-legged stop in front of the line of working pits. The horse was a quivering black shadow under the wan starlight, and the rider was a shadow proportionately huge and black.

With virulent curses, the rider urged the plunging horse in among the cowering overseers. He leaned far out of his saddle, cracking heads right and left with a fearful instrument —a knout, fashioned somewhat on the order of those used in Imperial Russia. Again and again the knout descended, its woven leather thongs, reënforced with wire and hardened by a rosin treatment, biting down deeply and forcing agonized yells.

One of the guards showed fight. He dodged the blow of the knout, flung in close against the plunging horse and reached up to pull the horseman from the saddle. The man in the saddle only laughed a raw ghoulish clacking, pulled a revolver from holster and shot the guard dead.

The horseman kept laughing and driving bullets into the guard's body, even after the fellow was slumped in a still, dead heap on the ground. After that, no one offered resistance.

The horseman raised his voice in a bawled order. Guards scurried frenziedly into the pits where Monk and Ham and Pat were shackled. They unlocked the leg irons and motioned for the captives to climb out of their holes.

The three were brought before the man on the horse. The man spoke in precise English. His voice was suavely sinister.

He said: "It was a stupid blunder of my slaves to chain you to the pits. It is only the Asiatic immigrant ships sailing to South America that I intercept for my pit laborers. Those, and occasional Ecuadorian fishermen, guano and moss hunters. When, upon rare occasions, a yacht comes this way, its occupants are received as welcome guests."

"How does a guest get off this island after his ship is wrecked?" Ham asked dryly.

"My dear General Brooks," came the precise voice from the darkly-bulking figure on the horse, "none have ever gotten off."

"This lug knows who we are!" Monk muttered. Then, aloud, he said: "They're all on here now, the guests?"

"They are, my dear Colonel Mayfair, though a bit unrecognizable, some of them."

Monk bristled. "Johnny better be recognizable."

"Doubtless you have reference to Professor Littlejohn," the other murmured. "He is quite recognizable. I shall take you to him. But first permit me to introduce myself. I am Count Alexander Ramadanoff."

Turning to the guards, the count barked an order. Men padded forward with peculiar contrivances, resembling wicker hammocks. They deposited the litters on the ground and stood a little back.

The count's hand waved out. His sardonic voice sounded: "There is one for each of you. Recline, and I will conduct you in state to the palace."

Monk hooted, "No hospital cot for mine. I'll walk!"

"Recline," the count ordered again, and the knout swung menacingly in his hand.

They took their places on the wicker litters—Monk grumbling, Ham doubtful, and Pat frankly grateful for the convenience.

"Hey!" Monk blurted. "We're forgettin' Habeas Corpus."

"You have reference to the trained Arabian pig?" the count questioned with suave politeness.

"You know everything, don't you?" Monk growled. "Yeah, I mean my pig."

Count Ramadanoff exchanged a few guttural phrases with the overseers, then addressed Monk.

"The pig must have escaped into the jungle. He will find company more to his liking there. Wild swine overrun this island."

Ham said, "Well, anyhow, we've seen the last of that hog."

Monk glowered at Ham. "It's your fault, shyster. *You* let him go."

"If it wasn't for you and your pesky pig, we wouldn't be in this fix," Ham retorted.

Count Ramadanoff cut short their quarrel by ordering the litter bearers to proceed. Through a narrow path hacked in the vine-matted jungle growth, they jogged along, the count, on his horse, bringing up the rear.

They came out on a strip of rocky coastline and the "guests" stared with astonishment.

"Blazes!" Monk gulped. "Blazes! Look!"

Rising sheer, washed by ocean spray on one side and bathed in the blood-red glare of volcanic light on the other, a palace of medieval Slavic type flung its black rock turrets high above the jungle growth.

Through a drawbridge in the bastioned wall of twenty-foot thick volcanic rock, they entered the bleak palace courtyard. The drawbridge swung ponderously closed behind them.

Pat shivered. She felt as though she was locked out of the world.

"An army couldn't get through these walls," Ham reflected uneasily.

"Some joint," Monk mumbled.

Past the high buttressed towers the "guests" were carried and deposited in front of a low-arched doorway. The count dismounted from his black horse and waved them inside.

"Some joint is right!" Monk said emphatically, as he stopped inside the stone threshold and stared around.

The room was huge, high-vaulted—an oppressive cavern of black volcanic rock and wooden beams. Demoniacal blue flames leaped within a fireplace large enough to have engulfed a whole ox for roasting. The fire shadows swooped on long curtains of somber ruby red which hung on brass hoops. Silver samovars glowed dully from shadowed recesses. Ancient icons looked down from the walls. The only modern touch in the whole vast room was a grand piano draped with costly sea otter furs and brightly illuminated by crystal-spangled candelabras which shed a yellow light from high overhead.

Count Ramadanoff indicated ornately gilded, ruby-plush chairs. "Sit there before the fire," he invited, "while your chambers are being prepared."

In the light, the count was revealed as a magnificently proportioned man, broad-shouldered, muscled, well over six feet in height. He was dressed in black—black riding boots, black breeches, black coat, black satin string tie. His Czar-of-Russia beard was black too, and his black eyes smoldered with a sinister light which it was impossible for him to conceal.

Pat sat on the edge of her high-backed chair and mentally chewed her finger nails because there had been no opportunity for her to divulge to Monk or Ham the information she had learned regarding the New York address of the count's brother.

Monk pawed at his bargelike jaw. "Where's all the other guests you mentioned?"

"Where's Johnny?" Ham rapped.

Pat also spilled questions. "What is the location of this island? How did you know us? Why did you wreck us? What are those horrible pits for?"

The count stood with his back to the fireplace, his fingers writhing before the blue flames, which, strangely, gave off little light and almost no heat.

"Answering your questions in order," he said in his suave, precise voice, "you would not enjoy seeing the guests."

"Why?" Monk demanded.

"Because, my dear Colonel Mayfair, most of them are in various stages of decomposition."

"Huh?" Monk grunted.

"The mortality rate among my guests has been regrettably high."

MONK went directly to the point. "You mean you kill 'em?"

"Nothing so crude as that," the count denied. There was a quality about the count's voice which gave a menacing, blood-crawling emphasis to his most casual words.

"What, then?" Ham demanded.

"They were, shall we say, liquidated."

"Sent to the pits?"

"Many of them, yes."

"Why?"

Fires flared deep in the count's fanatic eyes. "Some of them for trying to escape. Some for becoming too curious."

The man's cruel, glinting eyes fastened upon Pat. "For becoming too curious," he repeated. "That, I think, my dear young lady, answers all four of your questions."

Pat's breath drew in sharply. She glanced nervously around the oppressive room. "That's a beautiful piano," she said.

"It is, indeed," the count agreed. "Four men were killed taking it off the boat. Do you play?"

"No," said Pat. "Won't you play something?"

Count Ramadanoff nodded. "I regret to say that, later, I most likely shall."

"You regret?"

"Yes. When I play, it is always a prelude of unpleasantness for somebody. Savages in the jungle are aroused to an animal frenzy through the beat of their own tom-toms. In similar fashion, I am impelled to unspeakable decisions when my fingers wander over the keys."

Monk and Ham, playing a waiting game, said nothing.

Count Ramadanoff spoke again: "I have now met all except two of Doc Savage's world-famed specialists. It would give me the utmost pleasure to match wits—and strength—with this almost fabulous personage, Doc Savage, himself."

"Perhaps," murmured Pat enigmatically, "you shall."

A dark-skinned man approached on soundless feet, bowed low before Count Ramadanoff and motioned toward the broad stone steps disappearing upward in a sweeping spiral into a region of shadows and ruby-colored velvet drapes.

The thin, cruel line of the count's mouth seemed not to move, but an abrupt hissing noise escaped his lips. It seemed to be a signal of dismissal, for the slave turned and padded swiftly up the stairway.

"Follow him," the count said, shortly. "He will conduct you to your chambers."

UPSTAIRS, the three were shown to separate rooms.

Ham had not been alone for more than forty seconds before he saw his door latch lift noiselessly. He crouched, the fingers of his right hand involuntarily clenched, as though he gripped his deadly sword cane.

But the cane would have been of no use to him. It was only Pat who opened the door and eased into his room. In a rush of whispered words, she told him of her conversation with the pit guard who had been with Johnny's expedition.

"The logical place for the radio room is in the top of the tower," Ham said, excitedly.

"But there's a steel door barring the stairway to the tower!"

"Let us go talk to Monk," Ham suggested.

When he heard the news, Monk, characteristically, was all for immediate action.

"We won't get a better chance than now," he declared. Ham was inclined to agree.

"But that steel door!" Pat protested.

"Come on. We'll go look at it."

Monk eased out into the gloomy hall. For all his simian bulk, he moved with surprising agility on catlike feet. Pat and Ham followed.

"An army tank couldn't push it in," Monk muttered.

Monk reached the door, felt over the steel panels with his powerful hands. The door was tight in its frame.

Pat reached up and touched the latch. The door swung open soundlessly.

"Unlocked!" Monk blurted. "Well, I'm a bush ape!"

"Didn't I always say so?" Ham accorded, readily.

"You tailor's dummy," Monk retorted.

"*Sh-s-sh,*" Pat cautioned. "We may never get another chance at this. Come on."

The steps coiled upward, like a circular stairway in a lighthouse. They were fashioned out of blocks of untrimmed stone. There was no railing, no light. A single misstep on the narrow flight would plunge a person down to unknown depths.

Closing and bolting the door of ponderous steel behind them, they mounted single file in the pitch blackness, feeling with their hands, hugging the damp side wall.

They came out at the top in the tower room without mishap. A single alcohol lamp, set in a wall niche, burned with a small straight flame, casting a glow over the rock-girt room. The floor was constructed of steel plates. This room was as weirdly unreal as the rest of the place.

But there was nothing unreal about the banked instrument which glinted softly in the light. Ham and Monk pressed forward, their hands touching familiarly the tubes, condensers, wire-wound induction coils of a radio sending set as modern as any they had ever seen.

They switched on the juice and started tapping out Doc Savage's call letters. Violet light flashed weirdly from the tubes.

Pat's face shone pale in the glare. "Won't they hear this noise downstairs?" she questioned.

"Not a chance," Ham said.

"Couldn't hear a cannon through these walls," Monk confirmed.

HAM sent the key dancing under his sensitive fingers, as he spelled out the words of the message. The message read:

PRISONERS ON FANTASTIC ISLAND IN GALA-PAGOS GROUP STOP CONTACT BORIS RAMA-DANOFF THIRTY THREE REDBEACH ROAD LONG ISLAND STOP GRAVE DANGER——

Unexpectedly, the harsh transmitter whining ceased. The key continued its frantic dance under Ham's deft fingers but the electrical power had been cut off; no further radio words were flung to the air.

And now, a new sound flooded the room. The sound came from everywhere, yet from nowhere definitely. It crept and crawled and writhed—never loud, but clear, insidiously penetrating, eerie, freighted with menace and unseen death, causing hair to tug at its roots and goose flesh to prickle out with a shuddering chill.

This sound which wafted with such horrible portent through the high tower room was music. Piano music.

"The count is playing his piano," Pat said in a small voice.

"He said he only played when somethin' was goin' to happen to somebody," Monk remembered aloud.

"How can we hear it from this high place?" Ham asked, tensely.

"This radio apparatus makes more noise than a piano," Pat said, fearfully. "If we can hear him, he must have heard us!"

Ham said grimly, "It must be *because* he heard us sending the radiogram that he's playing on his piano."

Suddenly the music stopped; but the notes continued to throb their eerie menace for seconds, it seemed, before quietness clamped down.

"Let's get out of here!" Monk jerked, breaking the ominous hush.

"Do not be in a hurry," a suave voice interposed.

It was Count Ramadanoff who spoke. No one having heard that sinister voice before could have mistaken it. The prisoners stared helplessly, trying to locate it.

Then a huge slab of stone in the tower wall swung outward. From within a hidden recess, the count stepped forth. He carried a modern automatic pistol in his hand.

"I always plan my radio room with two entrances," he purred. "And dictaphones are useful household articles to one such as I. And now, since you have violated my hospitality, I must dispense with your valued company. You are, accordingly, sentenced to labor in my pits. Strong-backed coolies sometimes last a month. A big Frenchman, last year, endured for two weeks——"

Monk's hand thrust down and squashed out the feebly flaming alcohol lamp. In the pitch darkness which flooded the tower room, he hurled the glass lamp bowl at the spot where the count, revolver in hand, had been.

At the same instant, all of Monk's great muscles acted to wrench his body to one side. The action undoubtedly saved his life. Saffron gun flame and a bullet blasted out of the count's revolver. The lead slammed so close to Monk that it jerked a quick breath from his lips.

A loud curse from the count indicated that the man had been struck by the flung lamp. Both Monk and Ham leaped forward in the darkness to overpower him before he could recover from the blow. But not more than a single step did they take. Then a blighting force seemed to rocket through their bodies.

Pat, also, felt the enervating force. It tingled from the feet to the tips of the fingers, freezing the muscles into instant, cramped immobility. As firmly as though they were glued to their tracks, their feet were fastened to that steel-plate floor. They could only tremble; they could not cry out.

A WHITE beam slashed from the count's flashlight. He barked an order and out of the same secret entrance through which he had originally appeared, a shadowy man-figure emerged. The man moved silently and slapped handcuffs on the wrists of the three.

The count reached back and turned off an electrical switch. The numbing force which held the prisoners fast to the floor flowed out of their bodies again, and they were free to move.

"As you must have deduced," the count's suave voice sounded from beyond the flashlight, "these steel floor plates, in alternate strips, are wired to take charges of electricity. You were rooted to the floor by the electrical current as efficiently as though you had sat on an electric railway track and grasped the third rail. I, myself, as you see, am wearing sandals insulated by thick rubber, and so am immune to the shock."

He paused impressively.

"I have just one thing more to say," he continued. "In view of your belligerent attitude, I have decided not to send you to the pits, but to keep you here in the palace under my close observation. Kindly proceed down the stairs and we will join another member of your group: Professor William Harper Littlejohn—or Johnny, as I believe you refer to him."

Near the bottom of the winding stairway, the count requested his prisoners to halt. He indicated a long slot in the tower wall, which looked out upon an inner courtyard. Hemmed in as it was on all sides by starkly-rearing palace walls, the courtyard was, in effect, a dungeon pit. A dozen feet above the flagstoned yard, a balcony ran entirely around it.

"Under the balcony," the count's voice sounded in a silky purr, "observe your new quarters."

They looked. Thick iron bars extended from the balcony edge into the flagstoned floor below, marking off a number of bare prison cells.

Count Ramadanoff spoke again. "Do you observe that bundle of rags in the cell off to the left? Look closely."

While they strained their eyes in the courtyard gloom, the interminable red lightning rippled out of the island volcano and sent its ghostly glare over the heavens. Cleverly arranged reflectors at the top of the courtyard dungeon directed the hellish glow downward to the flagstoned floor.

The still bundle of rags in the barred cell was bathed in the blood-red light.

"Johnny!" Monk and Ham jabbed, fiercely.

And Pat echoed it: "That's Johnny in there!"

"You will be interested to know," the count's odious voice continued, "that the cell bars are movable. They are actuated electrically. I have only to press a button, and they rise out of the floor to allow a prisoner to step out into the courtyard—or to allow the prisoner to be visited by an inhabitant of the courtyard."

"What inhabitant?" Pat asked quickly, impelled by a foreboding curiosity. "I don't see any." But the next instant she did.

A bulky shadow stirred from the flagstones, propelled itself out into the red volcanic glare.

Pat gave a little choked cry of sheer horror, and started back. Ham leaned forward, his fingers clutched so tightly on an imaginary sword cane that the knuckles were white splotches on his skin. Monk crouched, his simian bulk frozen.

"Blazes!" he gulped.

The courtyard below had an incredible inhabitant. Monk, Ham and Pat, all three, possessed what is commonly called an "iron nerve." Yet the thing below aroused in them absolute horror, a feeling of desperation. They seemed hardly able to breathe as they stared at it.

"It ain't real!" Monk choked, at the same time knowing he was mistaken.

"It is quite real," murmured the count.

They stared, as fascinated as birds suddenly confronted by a snake. Suddenly, Pat emitted a low, strangled cry, spun, covered both eyes with her hands. She trembled.

"Your chief, this famous Doc Savage," the count droned, "would no doubt be greatly interested by our little friend in the courtyard."

Chapter IV

RADIO TRAP

As a matter of fact, some very interesting things were, at that moment, on the point of happening to Doc Savage.

In the skyscraper section of midtown New York, a man so thin that at first glance he seemed to be walking sidewise, and who had a skin so white that it rivaled the pallid waxiness of a lily, strode along with a briskness which belied his fragile physical appearance.

The man—"Long Tom," or Major Thomas J. Roberts, electrical wizard, as he was known to the world at large—was another of Doc Savage's aids. Long Tom's specialty was electricity, of which he had profound knowledge. Electrical patents recorded under his name were legion.

Long Tom looked like a man on his last legs. But appearance in his case was a terrific lie. His chalk-white face did not indicate ill health. He happened to be one of those rare individuals who, no matter how much they expose themselves to the sun's rays, cannot get a tan. There was incredible strength in his fragile-appearing body.

Long Tom turned in at a building which towered, a sheer mountain of gleaming stone and steel, nearly a hundred stories into the sky. The entire eighty-sixth floor of this building constituted the New York headquarters of Doc Savage.

Past a phalanx of elevators in the skyscraper lobby, Long Tom strode, and paused before Doc Savage's own private elevator shaft, fishing in his pocket for a key. This speed elevator was of Doc Savage's own ingenious designing, and it maintained lightning passage between that eighty-sixth floor and the main lobby, as well as the basement where, in a subterranean garage, Doc's remarkably equipped motor vehicles were housed.

Fitting the peculiar key to the hole, Long Tom gained access to the speed elevator.

He jumped wildly just after he stepped into the lift. There was blurred movement as something—it appeared to be an amazingly elongated mouse—scurried between his feet and disappeared around the corner in the lobby.

Long Tom popped his head out of the elevator to get a better view. All he got was another impression of blurred motion. The thing, strangely, did not seem to be running on legs, nor did it writhe like a snake. It flowed, seemingly.

Like a grayish-blue streak it flowed against the shiny black oxford of a uniformed elevator starter and disappeared within the recesses of his trousers leg.

The elevator starter was an active young man, who liked to practice tap steps when no one was around. He was rather good at it. But the dance routine he went into when that grayish-blue streak flowed up his pants leg was like nothing executed on a stage or ballroom floor.

Long Tom grinned at first, watching the young man's epileptic antics. But suddenly he quit grinning and started forward with great strides.

He had caught a glimpse of the elevator starter's face. The young man's features were knotted in stark agony. A shrill cry broke from his writhing lips. His knees bent under him. He fell, arms gyrating wildly.

Long Tom caught him before he struck the floor and bent over the shuddering body, his hands patting frenziedly over the young man's trousers leg, attempting to crush that unseen thing responsible for the fellow's tragic condition.

"STAND back," Long Tom warned, as men and women in the lobby surged close, curious.

They paid no attention, of course, crowding in and staring, asking aimless questions. New Yorkers invariably behave thus, when one of their number acts in a manner slightly deviating from the normal.

"Get a doctor," some one advised.

"Stand back," Long Tom warned again, sharply. "Something bit him. There's a posion snake, or bug, or rat or something, loose in here. You're all in danger!"

Even that did not move them. With new recruits continuously pressing in from behind, the crowd swelled closer. Curiosity was an emotion more rampant than fear.

Then something happened which did move them. They became all at once conscious of a man approaching. He neither spoke nor shoved, but there was such quiet mastery in his face and manner that, instinctively, they looked at him, and then with a kind of awe, pressed back to allow him free progress through the crowd.

The man was a giant. His strong features, kilned by tropic sun and arctic wind, and held under superb emotional control, seemed to be molded in bronze. He topped, by fully a head, every man in the lobby. And yet, so perfectly was his huge frame developed, prodigious muscles molded in perfect symmetry, that it was only the manner in which he towered above the close-pressed crowd that revealed him as the giant he really was.

His crisp hair seemed made of bronze only a shade darker than his skin. His great neck sinews, only slightly less hard than metal, showed decidedly above his collar. Cables of the sinew ridged his hand.

The most remarkable feature of all about the bronze man, was his eyes. Strange eyes they were, hypnotically compelling; like pools of flake-gold, stirred with restless life, as though tiny whirlpools kept the fine gold flakes continually in boiling suspension.

For an instant after the bronze giant was discovered in their midst, a hush settled over the lobby.

"Doc Savage!" some one said.

Others took up the name. From lip to lip, the murmur flew: "Doc Savage!" . . . "Doc Savage!"

DOC SAVAGE was bending over the unconscious form of the elevator starter. Cabled fingers which could, without exaggeration, twist a horseshoe into a straight line, rolled up the trousers leg of his patient with gentle deftness. On the calf of the leg, two rows of blued holes were revealed. There was no swelling, no inflammation, just that double row of tiny lacerations.

Suddenly, penetrating the many-mouthed murmur in the lobby, came a weird sound, a kind of musical trilling which ran up and down the scale, softly, fantastically, as though the sound emanated from the air itself. It was suggestive of the sibilant slipping of an evening wind through palm fronds, or of the call of some golden-winged bird out of an Arabian Nights fairy tale.

This sound came from Doc Savage himself. It was an unconscious part of the bronze man, a thing he did in moments of stress or at times of great surprise.

Doc Savage spoke to his aid, Long Tom. The bronze man's voice was arresting, deep, pleasantly resonant.

He said, with impressive simplicity, "We will take him upstairs."

Doc lifted the unconscious man with noticeable ease. The crowd made a path for them to the elevator.

On the eighty-sixth floor, Doc Savage and Long Tom entered the headquarters reception room. The room, with its great comfortable chairs, deep-piled oriental rug, solid table exquisitely inlaid with ivory, reflected the power and solid dignity of Doc Savage.

Doc examined his patient more closely and administered a hypodermic.

Long Tom hovered close. "Will he come out of it, Doc?"

"He will," the bronze man said, quietly.

Doc listened then attentively, while Long Tom related what he knew of the elevator starter's injury.

"Did you identify the thing which attacked him?" the bronze man queried.

Long Tom shook his head. "I only glimpsed it. It seemed to flow along the floor so fast, I saw only a blur. It didn't appear again, after attacking this lad. I think it must have been trampled under the feet of the crowd."

Doc pointed to the parallel rows of lacerations on the patient's leg. "Only one thing could have left such marks."

"Centipede?" Long Tom hazarded.

"Correct," Doc said. "Judging from the angle in which the anterior legs, or modified fangs, have dug into the flesh, and the space between lacerations, and the immediate effect of the creature's poisonous bites, I should say one of a species of giant centipedes indigenous to the Galapagos Islands."

"The Galapagos! That's where Monk and Ham and Pat sailed, looking for Johnny!"

"They have arrived," Doc said grimly. "And they found trouble."

Long Tom stared. "How do you know?"

"This message came in over the short-wave set, a few minutes ago."

Doc handed Long Tom a copy of Ham's and Monk's message, reading:

PRISONERS ON FANTASTIC ISLAND IN GALA-
PAGOS GROUP STOP CONTACT BORIS RAMA-
DANOFF THIRTY THREE REDBEACH ROAD
LONG ISLAND STOP GRAVE DANGER——

Long Tom whistled. "I'm beginning to get it! It's a long arm that reaches from the Galapagos to New York City. This centipede was meant for you, Doc! It was introduced into your elevator as an attempt upon your life."

"Perhaps," Doc Savage admitted, "though the immediate intent was probably to render me unconscious, as the first step in a kidnaping plot."

"How do you figure that?"

"A centipede's bite is rarely fatal. But we all seem to be under the thousand-legger's shadow. Consider: Johnny was first apprehended; now Ham and Pat and Monk are taken. And almost paralleling their message of distress, comes this Galapagos calling card in the form of a centipede."

Long Tom was silent for a moment. As a result of their unceasing war upon the most ruthless and cunning forces of criminal adventurers, Doc and his aids lived always in the shadow of danger. But at the moment, they had no active case under investigation. The developments of the last few minutes had struck with stunning suddenness.

"What do you make of it, Doc?" Long Tom questioned, uneasily.

"Frankly," said Doc, "I don't make anything. It's a complete mystery."

"That address in the radiogram; we ought to turn up a clue there."

Doc nodded soberly. "I was on my way to 33 Redbeach Road when I ran into the excitement downstairs. Let me suggest you see about getting this young man to his home, then jump in your car and join me at the Long Island address."

Doc descended in the private elevator to his subterranean garage, the existence of which was known only to a few people outside the immediate circle of his five aids. From among the number of specially built vehicles, Doc chose a low-swung coupe of gunmetal finish and expert streamlining. The car was, in reality, a rolling fortress, with bullet-proof glass, armored body, chrome-steel fenders, and bulletproof tires of cellular rubber construction.

The garage doors, actuated by photo-electric cells, opened slightly as Doc eased the car forward; the doors closed automatically behind him as he rolled along the ramp into the stream of uptown traffic. Toward Queensboro Bridge and Long Island he headed, the powerful motor under the beetle-backed hood propelling the car with silent, flowing motion.

SEEKING 33 Redbeach Road took Doc Savage to a semideserted tide-flat region on Long Island Sound. He turned in at a brush-grown lane. Swirls of fog were rolling in from the Sound. An ancient brick house with sagging porch roof and rusted rain spouts loomed through the mist. The place had evidently once been a fine estate, but it gave every evidence of having been deserted for a long time.

Doc parked under a dragging-branched elm which dripped water from leaves sodden with condensed fog. He did not get out on the steering-wheel side of his car. He slid over to the opposite side, stepped to the ground and disappeared in a grove of wet birches.

Doc had no reason to doubt the authenticity of the Galapagos radiogram. He was not expecting trouble. But it was his policy never to take unnecessary chances.

After a few minutes of reconnoitering, he approached a side entrance to the decaying mansion and knocked. There was a long silence. Doc knocked again. Still nobody came.

Doc Savage, through years of patient training, had perfected his hearing to an animal keenness; he could hear sounds above and below the scale audible to the average person. Within this house which appeared to be as deserted as a snatched grave, he could hear movement—hurried, secretive, man-movement.

Doc's bronzed features remained immobile. He simply waited there by the door, and after a while the knob turned from inside the curtained room and the door opened. A foreign-appearing man with short-cropped hair stood within the dimly lighted interior and invited him in.

"You are Doc Savage?" he questioned in broken English. "I have been expecting you. I am Boris Ramadanoff."

Doc stepped inside, but, because he had been made wary, the thing which happened next was no surprise to him. With all his senses alert, he caught the creak of shoe leather against the carpeted floor, the virtually imperceptible movement behind a curtained alcove.

The bronze giant crouched and whirled, as men flung in at him from three directions. His cabled hands streaked out, closing with a grip of iron on the shoulders of two of his attackers. He lifted them both from the floor, crashed them against each other and let them drop.

They fell, stunned, in an octopus tangle of arms and legs; and Doc, with smoothly synchronized effort, struck out with his appalling fists at two other of his attackers.

Just once with each fist, he struck. One man went down, wailing, his face altered. The other, jarred into instant unconsciousness, went down, too, and never knew until an hour later that his jaw was broken.

Doc swerved as he caught a glint of the revolver drawn by the man with the cropped hair who had represented himself as being Boris Ramadanoff.

With a leap that in its force and precision could be compared only to that of a Nepal tiger, Doc landed halfway across the room. The short-haired man smacked the floor with a solid thud, and Doc was standing there with a firm grip on the revolver.

He was absolute master of the situation. There were ten men in the room besides himself. Most of them lay stunned as the result of Doc's rough handling; the others cowered back, afraid to try another move.

From outside the house, in the direction of the roadway, sounded a burst of machine-gun fire. Echoes crashed flatly. Then a new noise broke with a harsh drumming. It was a fearful sound. Doc Savage recognized it as the bullfiddle bellow of one of the superfiring pistols carried by his aids.

The superfirer was one of Doc's inventions. It resembled an overgrown automatic, and pumped out a withering stream of so-called "mercy bullets," hollow shells filled with a drug which, upon the slightest penetration of the skin, produced instant unconsciousness. It was Doc's code never to take a human life when he could in any way avoid it.

Wafting on the hooting echoes of the superfirer, came a sharp, urgent sound of a man calling.

"Doc! Doc!"

The bronze man recognized Long Tom's voice. He could guess what had happened. Long Tom, according to directions, had driven up and he had run into a machine-gun ambush as he stepped out of his car. Fierce fighter that he was, Long Tom would never call for aid unless the emergency was dire.

The safety of his men was a thing that Doc Savage put before every other consideration. On the instant, Doc gave up the advantage which he held over his enemies in the room. He wheeled, wrenched open the door, and plunged out into the fog, his great thewed legs carrying him in giant strides to Long Tom's aid.

Doc still held the automatic which he had taken from the man who had said he was Boris Ramadanoff.

Doc Savage carried no revolver or superfirer of his own. It was the bronze man's contention that dependence upon such a weapon robbed a man of ingenuity, made him helpless

in the face of danger should he chance to be deprived of
the accustomed weapon. Therefore, Doc depended upon his
own strength and cunning to pull him out of desperate
situations. Where strength did not suffice, he resorted to some
chemical or mechanical trick, which was usually effective
and always baffling.

Doc did not scorn the use of a gun, of course, when
emergency put one in his hands. He used one now. Pushing
out through the dripping birch leaves, he came upon Long
Tom who, behind a meager rock shelter, was caught in a
threatened cross-fire of submachine gun lead.

As the machine gun swiveled down to rake Long Tom,
the automatic in Doc's hand barked. The single bullet damaged the hand of the gunner. The man squalled and let his
weapon clump to the ground. The second machine gunner
swung the snout of his death-dealing gun on Doc, holding
down the trigger, slicing a leaden pattern through the fog-
drenched birches.

But the gun cut out before the leaden stream reached Doc.
Another coolly directed bullet from the bronze man's automatic took care of that. The gunner cursed, let his weapon
drop and wrung his injured hand.

From behind the brick house, now lost in the fog, sounded
the throaty roar of two automobile motors exploding into
life. There was a grinding of gears, clashing shifts into
second, then a rapidly diminishing sound as the cars rammed
into distance.

"Watch this pair," Doc called to Long Tom.

Doc's prodigious strides carried him in a matter of
seconds back to the house. As he had feared, all ten of his
attackers were gone. He searched the house. It was empty.
The uninjured men had loaded the unconscious members
into the cars and decamped.

Doc did find one thing—a hastily scrawled note, signed:
"Boris Ramadanoff." The note read:

Next time it will be different. We will use more
than our fists.

Long Tom came up with the two prisoners.

"Stay here and watch this place," Doc directed. "Move
your car up close to the house, where we can keep in
touch with each other through the short-wave radio set while
I tail those vanished cars."

But Doc did not chase the autos. The bronze man's coupe,

each car used by his aids, and their eighty-sixth floor head-quarters as well, was fitted with short-wave telephone receiving-and-transmitting apparatus. As Doc flung inside his car, he clicked concealed switches under the dash.

Static crackled from the radio loud-speaker, and then the excited voice of Colonel John Renwick, renowned engineer, the fifth of Doc's five aids, boomed out of the diaphragm.

"Renny" was doubtless speaking from the skyscraper headquarters.

Doc lifted a microphone from a concealed hook. "Listening," he said.

Renny's voice roared: "Better get back to headquarters quick, Doc. There's the devil to pay!"

Chapter V

RUSSIAN TEA PARTY

As the bronze man hurled his car down the driveway, he spoke back through the microphone—the radio apparatus functioned while the car was in motion, of course.

"What, precisely, has happened?" he asked over the air.

Renny's voice bawled out of the loudspeaker: "That queer centipede that disappeared after clawin' up the elevator starter—well, it showed up again."

"Did you manage to kill it?"

"Yes, but too late. It attacked another man."

"Yes?"

"The man died, Doc!"

"Are you positive the victim was killed by the centipede's bite? Except in the case of the aged or infirm, death rarely results from——"

"Nothing aged or infirm about this victim, Doc. He was a thirty-year-old, two-hundred-pound cop, and he took about six breaths—that's all—after the bug got him, and died in my arms."

"That was too quick for a hypodermic to have done any good. Watch yourself, Renny."

Doc spoke quietly, but Renny understood that the bronze man had delivered a warning that an ordinary man would have yelled.

"Is there anything else?" Doc Savage questioned.

"No—except there's a guy here waiting to see you."

"Who is he, Renny?"

"Some Russian-sounding name—Boris Ramadanoff."

From his radio speaker, Renny heard a weird note—an almost soundless musical trilling. He thought it was some static manifestation at first, but almost instantly he identified the sound as that subtle emanation peculiar to Doc Savage in moments of stress or surprise.

"Doc," Renny thumped, "what is it?"

The bronze man countered with a question of his own. "How long has Boris Ramadanoff been there?"

"Long as I have, anyhow—ten minutes."

"Describe him."

"Old-fashioned little guy with a black cutaway coat and a black Czar-of-Russia mush all over his map. Talks with an accent. What's the excitement, Doc?"

Doc complied: "A man claiming to be Boris Ramadanoff sought to kill me, a few moments ago. Sit tight, Renny. We have good reason to believe that the lives of Johnny and all those who went after him—maybe our lives, too—depend upon what we do within the next few hours."

As Doc stepped out of his elevator on the eighty-sixth floor and entered the headquarters reception room, a remarkable man shifted his towering bulk out of a comfortable leather chair and lumbered forward. Alongside any one but Doc Savage, this individual would have been considered enormous.

This man had a long, puritanical face that was shrouded in gloom, as though he had lately returned from a funeral and contemplated going to another. As a matter of fact, the expression was habitual whenever he was expecting action, which was most of the time. Queerly enough, it meant he was happy. His fists swung restlessly at his sides. Huge fists they were, larger than Monk's, rivaling the flint-padded claws of a Kadiak bear.

The big-fisted man was "Renny"—Colonel John Renwick —an engineer who had possibly built dams and bridges in more parts of the world than any man alive—and knocked out more door panels with those appalling fists.

Renny's hand waved toward a little man who had sprung up from a chair and was in the middle of a courtly bow.

"This is Boris Ramadanoff," Renny announced.

The black-bearded little man continued to make bows. "I am prostrated," he said in precise English. "From the colonel here, I have just learned that you met with trouble from a man posing as myself."

"Do you have an address on Redbeach Road?" Doc asked, cryptically.

"But yes! The number is thirty-three."

"Within the last hour at that address, several men, one

of whom claimed to be Boris Ramadanoff, did try to trap me," Doc admitted.

The little man's eyes gleamed. "Was he a bullet-headed fellow with close-cropped hair?"

"The one who claimed to be Ramadanoff? Correct."

"I know of him. I repeat it, sir, I am prostrate! To think that you should be set upon by thugs in my own home! The truth is, I have many enemies. Doubtless they took possession of my house, their intent being to apprehend you, in the belief that you could furnish them with information regarding my whereabouts. Accept my most profuse apologies."

Doc nodded. "You wished to see me?" he suggested.

"From South America, I have come to see you!" The little man bowed again, and with a quick, birdlike motion thrust a leather folder toward Doc.

"THIS establishes your identity," Doc said to Boris Ramadanoff, as he handed back the papers. "And now——"

"I seek your aid, sir," Boris said earnestly. "I need it desperately. Lives hang in the balance. I will come quickly to the point. In the Galapagos Archipelago there is an unknown island upon which my brother, the Count Ramadanoff, has set himself up as master of life and death over every living thing, causing ships to be wrecked, and forcing the seamen to dig the circular pits."

"Why the pits?" Doc questioned.

Boris shrugged eloquently. "That is a profound mystery to me. The Count Ramadanoff, my brother, transported all his worldly possessions from our native land to this island before the revolution. He brought with him artisans who built a castle. But of that original company, I alone remain. He has killed them all. His real motive for such horrible deeds, I do not know."

"Precisely what do you want of me?"

"I want you to go with me to that island in the Galapagos and help free scores of poor devils—shipwrecked seamen—digging their way to death in the honeycomb pits."

"Purely an appeal in the name of humanity?"

"Yes; although, in freeing those others, you may also be in time to save one of your own men, Professor William Harper Littlejohn, who is also a shipwreck victim of my mysterious brother!"

The little man had meant this to be a smashing climax to his appeal. But, if he expected Doc to show surprise over the information, he was disappointed.

Doc said merely, "How do you know about this?"

"I was on the island at the time my brother caused your aid's boat to be wrecked. Since then, I escaped."

"You have come directly to me?"

"Yes—and thereby saved my life!"

"How do you explain the Redbeach ambush?"

"I arranged for the house some time ago, without seeing it, expecting eventually to make it my permanent New York address." The little man's eyes closed weakly. A shudder coursed over him, tremoring the very tip of his beard.

"My fiendish brother anticipates every move I make! His hand is long—and ruthless. He caused the trap to be set for me at Redbeach Road. He caused the centipede trap to be set for me here, thus bringing tragedy to those two: the policeman and the elevator starter."

Doc put another question to Boris Ramadanoff. "You have charts which will enable us to fly directly to the island?"

"But yes. They are at your disposal."

"How soon can we see them?"

"At your convenience. Immediately, if you wish."

"The sooner the better," Doc said.

Ramadanoff bowed. "My thought exactly. Perhaps you will be moved to accompany me now to my hotel apartment? We will go over the charts—perhaps plan a course of action—we will have tea."

Doc assented. As he and Ramadanoff were leaving, the bronze man advised Renny: "Best stay where you can keep in touch with Long Tom and myself."

In Ramadanoff's apartment—the apartment was like a thousand others in the metropolis—Doc sat studying charts, while Boris Ramadanoff, in the next room, brewed tea.

Soon the little man came out smiling. "The day for me is not complete without my tea. You will join me, no?"

Doc nodded shortly, and fired questions relative to directional bearings on the unknown island. The other answered concisely; then, excusing himself, he left the room and returned with a silver tray bearing two crystal glasses two-thirds filled with pale tea, and a steaming china-lined silver pot.

"Please," he said, holding the tray before Doc.

Doc took one of the glasses and touched his lips to it. There were two reasons why he did not drink more. One reason was that he did not commonly indulge in stimulants of any kind, reserving them only for their proper emergency use. The other reason was that his acutely developed taste warned him of a foreign substance in the tea.

"You do not care for it?" Ramadanoff asked, solicitously. "It is made in my own samovar which I carry with me always. But perhaps you do not like the flavor of the Galapagos herbs which I add to the tea to give it its unusual tang?"

Doc's gold-flecked eyes bored steadily at Ramadanoff. "It is not the herbs to which I object. It is the poison."

"What?" The little man's hands, holding the tray, started shaking so that tea splashed from the spout of the silver pot.

"Poison," Doc repeated.

"Poison?" Ramadanoff gasped, incredulously.

He sat the tray on a low table and reached out for Doc's glass. "Allow me," he murmured.

He raised the glass to his nose, sniffed cautiously. His face went white to the roots of his beard. The glass slipped from his trembling hand and crashed on the floor.

He slumped in a chair, then roused himself to lean forward and sniff at his own glass. He slumped back again, weakly.

"They are, indeed, poisoned!" he said hoarsely. "We have, sir, very narrowly escaped death."

"Do you recognize the active agent?" Doc asked, quietly.

"Yes, since you have called my attention to it."

"What is it?"

"A vegetable poison known, to the best of my belief, only to that Galapagos madman, my brother!"

Doc Savage continued to hide his reactions behind a mask of bronze immobility. "You can explain?" he asked.

Ramadanoff covered his face with trembling hands. Two gems on finger rings flashed a weird menace against his white hands. One of the gems was an emerald, thicker than a man's thumb. The other was a ruby of equal size and fineness.

"No," the little man moaned, "I cannot explain. As you yourself are aware, I left the room where I was preparing the tea for only a moment."

A new voice sounded, mockingly, in the still room. "The moment was ample!"

At sound of the voice, Ramadanoff stiffened in his chair as though an electric current had jolted through his body. He jerked his head from side to side, peering, with a groan, through spread fingers. He saw nothing to explain the mocking voice.

His writhing lips wrenched words.

"It is our doom—the Devil's Honeycomb!" He husked the meaningless phrase again: "The Devil's Honeycomb——" His tortured voice trailed into silence.

Only his long, tapered fingers moved, digging in agony into the flesh of his face; and the gems on his fingers protruded from the whiteness of hands like baleful eyes.

Chapter VI

THE PLATINUM PACKET

Doc's action, when that mocking voice filled the room, was in marked contradiction to Ramadanoff's. The bronze man sat perfectly still, relaxed.

Out of the dead hush, his voice sounded—controlled, compelling.

"Come and join our tea party," he suggested.

Another crawling hush followed Doc Savage's calm pronouncement. Then the closet door burst open. A man shouldered out, cuddling a submachine gun. The man was the same bullet-headed, hair-clipped individual who had posed as Boris Ramadanoff at 33 Redbeach Road.

While he kept Doc under the machine-gun muzzle, the man's guttural voice chopped orders, and two men, armed with automatics, sidled in from the next room and two more machine gunners came in through the French windows from the fire escape.

The five guns covered Doc and Ramadanoff in a close, deadly ring.

The bullet-headed man's blond face was a fiery red from the excitement of his triumph. His blue eyes glittered with cold malignity as he looked at Doc.

"I promised you," he gloated, voice thick with his foreign accent, "that, the next time, we would use more than our fists. And I promise you now that at the slightest sign of resistance, you will eat lead from five guns!"

"Interesting," Doc said quietly, remaining relaxed in the chair. "What do you want of me?"

The man with the close-cropped hair scowled. "*I'll* do the questioning. You figured we were here, didn't you?"

Doc nodded. "You made some slight sounds. And there

was your bodily odor, which carefully trained nostrils could detect."

The other snarled nervously, "Why didn't you do something about it, if you knew you were on a spot?"

Doc started stretching his arms, leisurely. "I intend to."

"The devil you do!" The machine gun jerked. The bullet head jerked, too. The thin lips barked an order. "Rats, the handcuffs! Get the big one first!"

A thin man with ratty eyes—one of those carrying an automatic—wrestled handcuffs from his pocket and approached Doc. He walked warily, his swarthy face apprehensive.

Doc, sitting in his chair, continued his leisurely stretching until his arms were straightened out from his body in the form of a cross. The rat-eyed man with the handcuffs stared helplessly, with panic gripping him as he found himself so close to those great, cabled fists.

"Don't go chicken, Rats," the bullet-headed leader snarled. "We can put enough lead in him to sink through the floor." To Doc, he ordered: "Hold your wrists together for the cuffs."

"All right," Doc said. "And when I do, you watch what happens."

Slowly, like the wings of an eagle closing, Doc swept his arms to meet in front of him. The eyes of every man in the room were on those closing arms. Doc meant that they should be. There was purpose in his dramatics.

While he was centering their attention on his arms, the toe of his right foot was deftly disengaging a novel metal packet from within his left trousers cuff. It was a packet scientifically designed to withstand the utmost in internal pressure, fashioned out of an alloy stronger than any other known metal.

The instant Doc succeeded in releasing the packet from the cuff, he kicked it away from him. The bullet-headed leader, alert for tricks, caught the movement out of the tail of his eye.

"Watch his feet!" he snarled.

It was too late for anybody to watch anything. A sharp, cracking explosion blended with an unnamable sound, a *sw-oo-sh* reminiscent of blanketing fire damp gas ignited in a coal mine. Almost instantaneously, the room was choked with a yellowish smoke so dense that it appeared black.

For the space of a rasped breath, there was silence. Then bedlam. Shrieked curses; splintering wood and crashing glass as automatics barked and machine guns clattered. In their panic at Doc's nerve-racking maneuver, the men butted blindly, their guns making ruddy flashes in the smoke as they drove their bullets.

Doc Savage was in the clear. At the instant of the smoke explosion, he had rammed forward from his chair, ducking low, one thewed arm reaching for the spot where he knew Boris Ramadanoff to be, the other arching upward like a scythe toward the bullet-headed leader's neck.

Doc's packet had contained an organic chemical held under pressure. With the bursting of the packet, the chemical had expanded instantly in a gaseous state. Moisture in the air had acted to cause partial combustion of the chemical, thus generating the instantaneous cloud of smoke.

Then the unexpected happened. Boris Ramadanoff was not where he should have been in the chair, and the short-haired leader had shifted his position.

Doc Savage moved about very silently, endeavoring to find Ramadanoff.

"Open the windows and let this stuff out," rapped the chief of the raiding party. "Everybody be perfectly still, so we can hear the bronze guy if he moves."

They could think quickly, these men. They had taken the one course which would most quickly result in disaster to the bronze man. Doc Savage changed his position, using the utmost stealth. Even his eyes could not penetrate the smoke.

Some moments passed in utter silence. Then, outside, police sirens began to wail in the streets. Neighbors must have heard the shooting, the excitement, and summoned officers.

"The cops!" ripped the man with the cropped head. "We gotta blow!"

With that, they made a concerted charge for the door. Doc Savage moved swiftly, but chanced to brush some one. There was a pale burst of gunfire and deep crash of gun noise near his ear. His hands streaked through the smoke, knocking the gun out of the man's grasp and clamping a hold on the fellow's neck.

There was more shooting in the room, wild shots.

"Out!" the mobleader was howling. "The law is comin'!"

Then, amid a great rush of feet, they were all out of the room. They slammed the door. A number of shots were driven into the panel from the hallway outside, to discourage pursuit.

Carrying the man he had captured under one arm, Doc Savage hurriedly searched the rooms.

Boris Ramadanoff was gone!

Doc Savage carried his prisoner to the fire escape, hurriedly descended. His purpose was to watch the rear of the apartment building. The police, by now, were around in front. They would take care of the entrance.

Doc Savage, noting that from the spot where he had parked his coupe he could watch the court that gave to the rear entrance of the apartment, hurriedly carried his prisoner to the car. It was just as well to get the fellow out of sight of the police, thus avoiding the delay which explanations would, necessarily, cause.

The radio was still turned on in the coupe. Static crackled from its loud-speaker, and mingled with that was the frantic crackle of words.

Doc recognized the voice. It was Long Tom, no doubt speaking from the transmitter of his car at the Redbeach Road address where Doc Savage had left him on guard. The electrical wizard's voice came in frantic bursts, almost inarticulate.

"Doc—centipedes—killing me——"

The words suddenly ceased coming.

That changed Doc Savage's whole plan of action. Any danger to Long Tom transcended in importance what might have happened to Boris Ramadanoff. Doc switched the coupe's engine on; with a squalling of tire rubber, it got under way. The car rocketed down the street, siren squalling. The use of the siren was permitted Doc by the police department. Doc depended upon it, of course, only in dire emergencies.

While he wheeled along, Doc called through the coupe's radio, attempting to renew connection with Long Tom; but he got no response.

He shifted his call back to Renny at headquarters. Renny was listening in, feverishly awaiting directions.

Doc said, "Better get over here to Ninety-seventh Street and stand by. Try to avoid trouble with the police. Leave your radio switched on in your car, so we can keep in contact."

"Right, Doc," Renny answered.

Doc replaced his microphone on the hook and turned his attention to the captive he had lugged into the car with him. He was "Rats" Hanley, the scrawny-chested, rat-eyed individual who had been going to clip the handcuffs on Doc.

Doc put pressure on him and learned from him that the bullet-headed man was Jans Bergman, and that Bergman worked for some one higher up. Gaining this information, Doc put Rats to sleep by pressing on a hidden nerve. Later, Rats would be sent to Doc's "crime college" in upstate New York. There, by surgical means, the crook would be cured of his criminal tendencies.

Doc's coupe crossed the Queensboro Bridge over the East River and continued along the Sound. Sea fog still hung heavy over the run-down estate, the decaying red brick house at 33 Redbeach Road, as Doc swerved his car in at the gate and rolled silently up the brush-grown lane.

There was no sign of Long Tom.

THE bronze man spent no time in reconnoitering. With Long Tom's life threatened, even seconds were important. He leaped from the car, traversed the short distance to the house in great bounds. He tried the door. It was locked. He used Renny's pet method, and one of his fists, propelled by prodigious arm and shoulder muscles, crashed through the solid oak panel.

Like closing vises, his hands caught the splintered wood and wrenched. He tore the door half down, then walked through the rest of it with forward-pressing force which shattered the entire door frame.

In the dim interior, he moved around. His footfalls sounded hollowly throughout the ghostly house. The place seemed to be deserted. He whipped out a flashlight, snaked its searing rays over floor and walls. Black corners leaped into white life.

In one room, he found evidence of a furious struggle. Furniture was overturned. Still-wet scarlet was on the carpet.

The crimson was not the most alarming thing. Scattered over the floor were the crushed bodies of fully a dozen centipedes. Hairy legs on some of the broken segments were still writhing.

While Doc's flashlight poked its white beam around the shambles of the room, there came a sound from the hall of a floor board creaking. Doc whirled, crouching a little, the light from his flash snuffing out.

He glided to the wall and waited, frozen close. The creaking from outside the door sounded louder. It paused, started up again, paused a second time within the doorway. Doc could hear the cautious breathing of the stalker.

The unknown took a wide step to clear the bare floor and land soundlessly on his feet on the carpet. He got his foot on the carpet, all right—then his whole body left the floor. With his feet as high as his head, he fell heavily on his back.

Doc had taken advantage of opportunity, when the stalker took his wide step, to pull the carpet from under him.

The man's trigger finger started jerking spasmodically. Plaster showered and the room rocked to gun thunder as orange flame stabbed the gray light. Suddenly, the echoing uproar stopped. There was a metallic clatter and a hollow thump. Doc, with one leap, had landed in the middle of the room, knocked the gun to the floor with one hand and whacked the man's head down with the other.

He looked at the man he had knocked unconscious. There was enough light to reveal features. The man was no one Doc had seen before.

But the next moment, Doc was looking upon a face which he *had* seen before. It was one of the few times in Doc's life that an enemy succeeded in actually surprising him.

A floor board creaked in the doorway. Doc looked up to find himself covered at deadly range with a submachine gun. The gunner had been able to advance without being heard because of the uproar the pistol shots had made.

The smooth skin of the man behind the submachine gun gleamed with pale menace in the half light. The wide mouth opened. Thin lips writhed in triumphant grimace.

The gunner who stood there threatening quick death was Jans Bergman, the man with the close-cropped hair whom Doc had left on Ninety-seventh Street, Manhattan, in an apartment with a squad car of the police department closing in.

"THERE is only one way you could have gotten here so soon," Doc said, quietly.

"One way," Bergman agreed, with his heavy foreign accent. "In the luggage compartment of your coupe."

"You are clever," Doc said.

"You had a lot on your mind," Bergman said grimly. "That helped. Stowed away in that compartment, I heard the radio S O S that came through from here."

"How did you leave everybody on Ninety-seventh Street?"

"Pretty badly shot up. It was a nice trick—the smoke. Your last trick, I think."

Doc straightened.

"Hold your hands high!" Bergman slashed. "Keep them wide apart! The fingers, even—keep them open."

Doc complied.

"And the feet—step them wide apart."

Doc moved to stand wide-legged.

"That's better," Bergman said. "You don't trick me this time."

Doc stared with a certain grimness into the slitted eyes of his enemy. He spoke what he was thinking.

"But few men have opposed me before, and risked another meeting."

"I," Bergman bragged, "am a bold man."

"Perhaps only foolhardy."

"You are the foolhardy one, if you think you can out-smart Jans Bergman. Maybe you're wearing bulletproof clothes. Don't depend upon them. My machine-gun lead will push your face out the back of your skull."

Doc shrugged, asked evenly, "Now that you have the bear by the tail, what do you propose to do?"

Bergman stared, slitted eyes glittering. "I'll keep holding the bear by the tail until—until a very few moments. Do you hear what I hear?"

Outside the house, an auto was droning up the driveway. The sound throbbed close, died. Car doors slammed. Feet scraped across the wooden porch, entered the house.

Bergman yelled, "This way, you guys!"

Foot scufflings, muttered curses sounded closer.

"Inside here," Bergman ordered. "Get a line on him from four angles. If he moves a finger a quarter of an inch, let him have it—in the face!"

Four men, black shadows in the gray gloom, eased inside the room and took positions within a yard of Doc, machine guns poking for his face.

Bergman bent, placed his rapid-firer on the floor, and approached Doc with handcuffs in one hand and an automatic in the other.

He said hoarsely, to cover his nervousness: "Now you will see how we treat the bear we have caught by the tail."

Something happened then and Jans Bergman was jolted by surprise greater than any which had come to him in his active life.

Doc Savage did not move his feet. He did not move his hands. He did not even move his fingers. But, suddenly, there was a sound that might have been explosion in slow motion.

There was superwhite light, too. It was an undertone of blue, and looking at it was something like looking at the arc of an electric welding operation. It did things to the eye. In fact, it brought blindness that was momentarily complete.

Doc Savage had his own eyes closed tightly, and thus

escaped the blinding effect of the flash to a great degree. He ducked for safety as lead spurted with ear-shattering clatter.

Jans Bergman began bellowing for his men to quit their suicidal shooting. More than any of them, Bergman came near understanding what had happened. He had caught the flash of Doc's wrist watch an instant before the flash came. He had realized the bronze man had expanded wrist muscles so as to split the case and release the contents.

Jans Bergman, of course, knew nothing of the chemical composition of the powder which had been in the watch and, when released into the air, had ignited instantly by spontaneous combustion. Nor did he know that the powder was one which, when burning—it burned like ordinary flash light powder—gave off those rays of light most destructive, over a temporary period, to the delicate nerve mechanism of the human eye.

While his enemies were milling about, cursing, shooting, gradually getting vision back into their eyes, Doc Savage plunged out into the hall. He slammed the door behind him, streaked through the shadowed house and outside into the sea fog which still rolled in from the Sound.

The bronze man made for his coupe in the driveway, got there in time to hear Renny's frantic voice trying to raise Doc through the loud-speaker. There was no way of telling how long Renny had been calling.

"Doc!" Renny was rumbling urgently. "Calling Doc Savage! Important!"

Doc grasped the microphone and said into the apparatus: "Listening."

"Doc," Renny thumped, "I am shoving off in my car—gonna join you. I've learned something. Boris Ramadanoff! Holy cow—he——"

A grinding crash blasted from the microphone.

It was a noise such as might have been made by two cars crashing together at high speed.

"Renny," Doc called in alarm, "are you all right?"

"All—right—Doc," sounded Renny's voice, faintly.

"Quick—what did you find out?"

A new voice jumped from the microphone, harsh, mocking. "The same thing you'll find out, Savage—after it's too late!"

Chapter VII

SUBWAY SEIZURE

Doc trod the starter of his car; but the great motor under its long hood did not throb into life. It remained as cold and unresponsive as the water-dripping trees which loomed through the fog.

He dived out and lifted the hood. He could see at a glance what was wrong. Wiring had been torn loose and ignition parts smashed. Jans Bergman, obviously, had used a monkey wrench before entering the house.

The gunfire had ceased inside the house. But it soon cracked from close outside. Lead skidded off the armor plate of the gunmetal coupe, mushroomed against the bullet-proof glass. Hoarse shouts sounded.

Doc Savage, a bronze flash, streaked from the other side of the car and melted into the fog. Bullets came hunting him, chopping through wet branches. Doc twisted, running low, changed his course, crashed on through fog-drenched trees and came out on the automobile highway.

A truck headed toward New York City pounded past. The bronze man left the ground in a headlong leap and got a grip on the endgate of the wheeling truck. He crawled over the gate and made his way forward.

From behind, he had been sighted by his enemies. Machine-gun slugs crashed out of the gray murk, but fanned harmlessly past as the heavy truck swayed around a curve. Doc reached the truck driver.

"Faster," he ordered.

The driver took one startled look and jammed the accelerator to the floor boards. The truck stepped up to fifty-five, weaving ponderously on the wet pavement. They covered a mile or two.

Fifty-five was not fast enough. At that speed, they could

be overtaken by Jans Bergman. A sleek sedan bored from behind, doing a few miles more than the truck. It was not Bergman. Just a motorist. As the motorist swung left to pass around the truck, there was a thump on his sedan which gave the driver a badly startled moment. A bigger moment followed for him when, unceremoniously, a door of his car opened.

Doc Savage had left the truck with a gauged leap, landing on the speeding sedan.

"Let me have the wheel," he ordered.

The bulging-eyed driver shot one gasping look at the bronze giant and complied. Doc took the wheel. The speedometer needle went to eighty—eighty-five—ninety miles an hour.

They were out of the fog now. Doc looked behind. There was a car tailing them. Doc recognized it. Jans Bergman's. The pursuing car was coming up fast.

They were running through traffic now. Doc did not want to subject pedestrians or his drafted driver to the dangers of speed and machine-gun bullets.

He said to the man who had been driving, "Slow down ahead there, I'm going to the subway station. I'm leaving you."

"O. K., D-Doc Savage," the other stuttered. He had recognized the bronze man. He would brag about this experience for the rest of his life. So would the truck driver.

The brakes squealed like stuck pigs, tires slithered, as the sedan buckled in toward the curb.

"Thanks," Doc flung, and plunged down the subway stairs.

A second afterward, Jans Bergman's car, rubber smoking, careened to the curb. Bergman stayed in the car, but three of his men burst out and followed Doc down the stairway.

THE automatic steel doors of a Manhattan-bound express train were sliding shut as the bronze man flashed through the subway turnstile. A split-second before the door hooks caught, Doc's outstretched hand fastened on the rubber-cushioned door edge and yanked the door open again. He disappeared within the brightly lighted car and let the door slide shut at his heels.

The doors to cars in New York subway trains are connected by a safety mechanism to the motorman's controls. When Doc stayed the closing of one door, it delayed the starting of the train. This gave Jans Bergman's men time to squeeze through the windows of another car.

The train started; it roared its way through the black tube.

The train was crowded. Passengers were standing closely packed in the wide aisle, some of them with hands reaching up to hold white-enameled grab-irons.

The cosmopolitan population of New York City is less observing, perhaps, than the citizenry of any other city in the United States. People crowd the streets, subways, towering skyscrapers of the metropolis with blank looks on their faces, immersed almost wholly in their own business. It is doubtful if even as commanding a personality as Doc Savage would have been noticed in the closely packed subway, except for the fact that the bronze man over-topped by a head the tallest man in the car.

People were beginning to murmur, to point, to gasp with recognition, when, suddenly, there was a crash of sound, a blinding swath of greenish-blue light enveloping the train.

With an ear-piercing shriek of brake shoes on wheeling metal, the train bucked to a violent stop, flinging many of the people in the car to the floor. Following the blinding greenish glare, darkness shut down—the darkness of underground places, jet and utter. Acrid smoke fumes drifted through broken windows, causing the panic-stricken passengers to shriek and struggle in mad frenzy against each other.

A uniformed trainman switched on a flashlight and bawled at the top of his voice: "There's no danger! Short circuit, that's all!"

The light was knocked from his hand by somebody's thrashing arm, but he kept on bawling to the milling passengers: "No danger! Take it easy! No danger!"

The New York underground is as safe as any railway in the world. The passengers knew this. Gradually the panic subsided as the hoarsely repeated words: "No danger!—No danger!" penetrated through the din to their consciousness.

FOR one person in that car, there was danger, however. This had been no ordinary short circuit. The unscheduled stop had been promoted by one of Jans Bergman's men. As the subway went back and the cars lurched to a standstill, Doc's great form was jostled to the floor with those others. But it was not alone the jolting car which had taken Doc off his feet. In the darkness, two hard swung blackjacks had thudded against his head.

Before the lights went on, under cover of the confusion, it was a relatively simple matter for Jans Bergman's thugs to lift Doc's limp body through a window and carry it down the black passageway. They cursed under their heavy burden and stumbled often, being careful to feel their way by scuffing their shoes along the cold rail at the opposite side of the track from the hooded death of the live third rail.

They came to a place where a red light glowed, marking an emergency exit in the massive expanse of dusty, reën-forced concrete. Onto the catwalk platform they lifted Doc, and carried him with effort up the steep steps.

Out on the street with their limp burden, they ran slam into a stick-twirling policeman. One of the men cursed under his breath and his hand jerked toward his coat pocket. Before he could draw his automatic, his quicker-witted companion had knocked his hand aside and blurted to the police-man:

"Subway accident—train stalled—this guy we're carryin' out overcome by gas! Lot more of them down there in the same fix. S'awful! You better report it."

Deceived, conscious of his importance in being the first to turn in a report of a first-page headline accident, the copper rushed for a call box.

Doc's captors rushed for a taxi, shoved the bronze man inside.

One of them clipped to the driver, "Nearest hospital." He spoke loudly, for the benefit of spectators crowding close.

IT was not in a hospital room that Doc opened his eyes. He was lying on his face on a brick floor, his wrists hand-cuffed behind him. He turned sidewise, maneuvered his legs under him, got to his feet. Light filtered wanly through a sidewalk grating, illuminating the bare, brick-walled room. The place was damp, musty-smelling. A single steel fire door, tightly closed, was the only exit.

Doc tried his weight against the door. His ramming shoulder attack shuddered the rusty sheet steel. With time, he might break through. Then he heard voices outside and paused, listening. He could not catch the words, at first.

While the muffled mumble of voices approached, Doc tried his strength on the handcuffs which bound him. Other times in his life, he had broken the connecting link on a pair of handcuffs by utilization of sheer strength and wrist leverage.

Muscles bulged and rippled now as he bent forward, exerting a terrific tug on the steel cuffs. He tried only once. Then he knew what he was up against. His enemies were taking no chances with him. His hands had been locked behind him with the most modern of tempered chrome hand-cuffs. A sledge and chisel would not have sufficed to get the cuffs off his wrists. It was work for a cutting torch.

Another appalling feature was that the cuffs contracted,

took up slack, when pressure was exerted against them, forcing a saw edge into lacerating contact with the wrists. Crimson dripped from his skin, where the steel points had gouged.

The bronze man bent his fingers upward till they could touch the end of his coat sleeve. His fingers moved deftly, unravelling a thread. From a pocket in the coat sleeve his hands received a small metal envelope, flexible as lead foil. Doc opened one end of the envelope with his finger nail and carefully maneuvered his hands to pour the liquid contents—a few drops only—on the handcuff links.

The talking men outside had now approached close enough to the door that Doc could hear what they were saying. He recognized one of the voices. It was Jans Bergman's. The blond, bullet-headed leader with the skull-tight skin had apparently just come in. His glib pronouncements sounded strange, when uttered with that foreign accent.

Doc heard him saying, "You left his clothes on? You fools——"

A sullen voice answered: "We frisked him—got everything he had."

"You couldn't have gotten half of it! Savage has a thousand pockets. You could yank out his teeth, shave his head, and pull out his nails and he'd still have enough chemicals hidden on him to blow up a battleship."

The other curved nervously. "I don't like it—monkeyin' with this bronze guy."

"You're getting your cut."

"What good's heavy sugar, if I croak before I can blow it?"

There was a silence, heavy, oppressive.

Then Bergman asked, "Has he come out of it yet?"

"Look through and see for yourself," the other snarled. "I ain't even lookin' at him any more. He's like a poisonous snake to me."

There was a sharp, metallic rasping as Bergman slid back an eye-slit in the door and peered through.

HE saw Doc lying on his back, feigning unconsciousness. "He's still out," Bergman said.

"He ought to be. We both of us give him a tap that would have busted a cable on Brooklyn Bridge."

There was another silence, more ominous than the one before. When Bergman spoke again, it was in a hoarse voice, curiously hushed.

"We've got to kill him," he said.

"Maybe you're right," the other muttered. "But how would

we kill him? A gunshot would bring one of them thousand-legged bugs crawlin' down our necks."

"A gunshot, yes—but a slit throat makes little noise."

"Get close enough to that bronze guy to cut his throat? Not for mine."

"He's handcuffed."

"Suppose he skins out of them cuffs?"

"How can he?"

"How can he do a lot of things he does?"

"All right, suppose he gets out of the cuffs? He can't; but if he does, look at the knives. We won't have to get so close to him as you're thinking."

Bergman tiptoed aside. From under a litter of boxes and excelsior packing he lifted two huge knives, bone-handled, with blades nearly half a foot in width and close to a yard long.

To Doc's ears came the gasped words: "Sugar cane knives, ain't they?"

"Right. I'm going to cut Savage's head off."

The heavy door swung open with ponderous creaking and Jans Bergman, followed closely by his companion, advanced across the damp bricks toward Doc's prone form. The assassins walked in a crouch, their machetes raised high.

ONCE in reach of Doc, they paused.

"If I don't make a clean job with the first stroke," Bergman muttered, "dip your own knife in the blood. Then follow me out in a hurry."

The other's teeth started chattering. The massive knife wavered and he grasped it with both hands.

"I'm practically out on the sidewalk now," he husked.

Bergman's knife lifted higher, then down it chopped, the wide blade glinting dully in the half light.

The first stroke was not enough. It was not even a starter. As the blade swished close, Doc, whose muscles had been tensely braced against the floor, wrenched head and shoulders forward.

It was too late for Jans Bergman to change his stroke. The frightful blade slammed past Doc's head and sank inches deep in the mortar.

Before Bergman could pull the blade free, before his companion could chop down with the other knife, Doc sprang an even greater surprise on them.

His arm, free from the handcuffs, struck out and down, against the back of the mortar-imprisoned blade, knocking it forcibly from Bergman's grasp. At the same time, his other hand streaked forward and grabbed the handle.

"No handcuffs!" the other man shrieked in terror, as he chopped down, holding his knife in both hands.

Doc parried the down stroke with the knife he had taken from Bergman. Steel met steel with grinding clangor, and the knife aimed at Doc skittered in the air, glinting like water heaved from a bucket, and clattered on the bricks at the other side of the room.

"No handcuffs!" Bergman echoed, and the skin was drawn so taut across his face in his terror at the spectacle of the bronze giant wielding that slab of razor-blade steel that it seemed his cheek bones must poke through.

The explanation of Doc's handcuff escape was simple. The liquid he had released from the flexible metal envelope had been an acid which made short shift of steel such as composed those handcuff links.

From outside the room sounded excited voices, approaching footsteps. Doc bolted for the door, brandishing his fearful weapon in the faces of the newcomers and scowling ferociously.

Doc made no attack on these enemies. He was looking for bigger game now. He took the basement steps in a series of bounds. From above, he hurled the unwieldy cane knife down, since he preferred to depend upon his own scientifically developed weapons.

Locking the solid door at the top of the landing and bolting it against the aggregation below, he stalked away in search of the master schemer he knew to be somewhere in the building; in search, too, of Renny and Long Tom, whom he surmised must have been captured.

It was this last objective which had brought Doc to this building. Back in the subway, the bronze man had not been knocked out by those thudding blackjack blows. He had only feigned unconsciousness, reasoning that the quickest way to locate his aids, if they were still alive, was to maneuver to get himself taken to their place of imprisonment.

Chapter VIII

THE THUMB-HOLE DEATH

MOUNTING from the basement, flight after flight, Doc Savage was not long in discovering the type of building he was in. It was one of those ancient tenements, condemned and abandoned, on the upper West Side of New York City near the Hudson River. It was a sore spot among the surrounding modern buildings, its windows blanked out with time-chipped whitewash.

As he raced upward, his senses were alert to catch the faintest sign of human habitation. His footfalls sounded hollowly against the worn, splintery floor, revealing wooden laths like the ribs of something long dead.

On the sixth floor, Doc paused. Here, plaster on the hall floor had been ground under many feet. Doc went up another flight. Here, too, plaster had been crushed underfoot. This building was several stories taller than most of its kind. Doc went up two more flights to the top floor, the ninth.

There were signs of recent passage on the stairway leading to the roof. Doc went up. At the top landing he had a mild surprise. A fire door of modern steel construction had recently been built in. It was solidly placed.

For the present, Doc contented himself with peering through a lookout slit in the door. His almost inaudible trilling sound, weirdly traversing the musical scale—that small, unconscious manifestation of Doc Savage in moments of stress or surprise—tremored in the dead air of early evening as the man of bronze focused his eyes on the roof top.

He saw a plane—a gyro of ultra-modern design—lashed down on the roof under a collapsible silk-cloth shelter. Huge silencers were attached to motor exhaust stacks. The roof had been leveled, patched and reënforced; and a raised apparatus—a navy type catapult—erected. There was also a conventional cable device to kill landing speed.

That the roof had been used for landings was evident by the wheelmarks. The district was a mercantile one, virtually empty after business hours. Surrounding buildings were low. Quite evidently, the gyro did not operate from this base by municipal permit, but it must have been able to go and come by night, undetected. Luminous paint markings on the roof were commencing to glow in the twilight. A clever scheme for night landings.

Doc turned, noiseless, a shadow in the failing light, and silently descended the stairs. On the sixth floor, he paused for a detailed search. Tracks in the plaster dust led to closed doors of several rooms. Before each door Doc paused, listening. He made no sound; he might have been a bronze, floating cloud.

Suddenly, a screeching, splintering noise crashed through the shadowed hallway—a screeching of hinges rent from doors, the splintering of the door itself under the terrific force of Doc's lunge.

Doc, listening in the hall, had caught the sound of human breathing inside the room. As he smashed through the door, a man who had been bending over, twirling the dials of a modern safe, straightened up with a guttural curse.

From the crashed-in door, all that was visible of the man was a bulky body, a blunt, close-cropped head. Jans Bergman!

IN the time it took for Bergman to jerk his bullet head around to look, Doc Savage had cleared the width of the room and locked a steel-thewed arm around the man.

Bergman struggled, trying to get at the automatic in his pocket. He was a big man; during his youth in his native country, he had won recognition as a wrestler. But, with Doc's arm holding tighter and tighter, strength flowed out of Bergman's body until, if Doc had not held him up, he would have fallen to the floor.

Doc appropriated Bergman's automatic and tossed it clattering onto the writing surface of an old-fashioned roll-top desk. Then he allowed Bergman to slump into a chair.

Doc indicated the safe. He said, "Greed brings many men to ruin. You did not leave when you had the chance. You came back here to help yourself to more money."

"Yes! Let's get out of here—while we're alive!"

Jans Bergman was staring up at Doc with panic creeping

into his slitted eyes. Sweat was beading his brow and glistening in the close-cropped hair on his head.

"Who is your boss?" Doc questioned.

Bergman's thin lips pressed so tightly they disappeared in the stretched smoothness of his skin. He shook his head.

Doc shrugged. "All right. But here is one you *will* answer. Where are my two men, brought here before me?"

Bergman's lips writhed. "I have nothing to say!"

Doc settled himself on the large roll-top desk, and said, "We will stay here until you talk."

"Savage, you're nuts!" Bergman jabbered. "It's as dangerous for you in here as it is for me! Sometimes a man drops dead with nobody near him, and what has killed him is a little hole in his temple about the size you could poke your thumb into."

"What makes that hole?" Doc queried, curiously.

"I don't know. But I'll tell you where your men are——"

In the twilight murkiness of the room leaped a peculiar sound, a kind of fleshy crunch. Bergman's words died in his throat. His head flopped sidewise. His shoulders followed it with flowing motion. His head thumped hollowly against the floor. His body lay there in a twisted huddle.

Doc leaped from the desk, made a quick examination. His fingers encountered a bone-crushed depression in the left temple, a smooth, white wound, in its size and contour the same as a man's thumb would have made if jabbed into white lard.

Even as Doc looked, the wound commenced to ooze scarlet in red pin points which quickly built up an overflowing red puddle. Bergman's flat ear divided the two streams, which ran onto the floor.

Jans Bergman's racketeering days were over. He was a victim of what he had called the "thumb-hole death."

A VOICE sounded in the room, precise: "The same thing could have happened to any one—any one!"

No one had come into the darkening room. There was no one standing outside the doorway. There was only that mocking voice rebounding from the walls.

Doc turned, fastened his gaze on the roll-top desk.

A laugh floated mockingly into the room. "Congratulations, my dear Savage. You have located my voice. Almost any second now you may look toward the doorway where you will be confronted by a second menace, not so mysterious, but fully as deadly as that thing which Jans Bergman so quaintly called the 'thumb-hole death'."

Shoe scuffling sounded from down the hall. Doc turned to see two men loom inside the doorway. They were clearly none of Bergman's men. They were squat Mongol types, massive of shoulder, heavy of jowl. They carried equally heavy, squat weapons—short guns with stubby barrels flared at the muzzle.

"Meet my personal bodyguard, Savage," the voice sounded. "Their weapons will interest you. They are instruments of my own designing, combing the features of a sawed-off shotgun and a blowgun. Each is loaded with slightly more than one hundred poisoned darts, which can be released *en masse* by a trigger controlling an air pressure mechanism. Your face will be the target, if you make it necessary for them to fire."

A faint whirring sounded and a stout oak panel in the side of the roll-top desk slid back. A man stepped out into the room, and the panel closed behind him. He stood there, with black glittering eyes—a little man with an Old World manner, and a black Czar-of-Russia beard.

It was Boris Ramadanoff.

Doc evinced no surprise.

Ramadanoff said, suavely, "Why should you wish to be here?"

"To secure the release of my two men."

As he spoke, the bronze man commenced sliding the toe of his right foot toward the cuff on his left trousers leg.

Ramadanoff's beady eyes caught the movement.

"Hold it!" he slashed angrily, and then in throaty Asiatic speech barked an order to his bodyguard.

The two squat assassins, Mongol eyes closing to slanting penciled slits in their broad faces, moved closer with their fantastic guns.

Ramadanoff warned Doc: "Twice you have escaped with your tricks. You will not do so a third time. The movement of a single muscle will bring you death."

Ramadanoff stepped forward, stooped, ran his fingers quickly around Doc's trouser cuff while the two Mongols held a steady bead on Doc's head with those wide-lipped guns. In the left cuff Ramadanoff's fingers closed on a small metal packet. He detached it with a quick movement and stepped back, holding the article as gingerly in his fingers as though it were a nitroglycerine cap. He deposited it upon the desk top, being careful not to allow it the slightest jar.

He faced Doc triumphantly. "Now, no more tricks. The claws of the tiger are drawn!"

The last words were spoken in a tone somewhat strange. They were jumbled, as if the tongue that made them was suddenly under the influence of an intoxicant.

Then the little man with the beard demonstrated that he was an amazingly quick thinker. As lightning strikes, so did the realization of something wrong hit him, and he acted simultaneously. Straight to the door he flung, to literally fall through it.

Doc Savage had been slightly crouched, waiting, knowing what was to come. The mechanism of the little packet was such that it would open shortly after being detached from his trousers cuff. It held some of the anæsthetic gas which he had developed long ago, and which he used so frequently —it was odorless, colorless, and its effects were almost instantaneous.

Doc lunged through the invisible gas. Holding his breath had saved him from the anæsthetic gas.

But where the door should have been there was something else. Doc collided with such force against an unyielding surface that he was flung back. He kept his breath in his lungs.

As firmly set as concrete, a smooth, metallic surface was now mysteriously substituted for the wooden door which he had bashed in with his fists. He heaved the full weight of his massive shoulders, ramming with all the power of his remarkably developed body. The surface did not budge.

From outside in the hallway, sounded Boris Ramadanoff's sardonic, if weak, laugh. His voice filtered in faintly. He had not gotten enough of the anæsthetic to overcome him.

"Just a trick, Savage," he snarled. "I managed to press a button on my way out, sliding the steel door into place from within the wall. Did you think I had no more protection for my safety than the wooden door you broke down? You can stay in there and simmer in your own juice, as the Yankees say, or perish in your own gas.

"I will go back and tell my brother it was a mistake for him to have sent me to New York for you. You cannot be controlled. Very well—then die!"

Chapter IX

FLAMING FURY

WHILE Ramadanoff's voice droned from the hallway, Doc turned. Three great strides carried him to the window. There was a grating sound that would have set a man's teeth on edge. It was caused by Doc Savage's finger tips scraping on smooth metal. The same mechanism which had blocked the doorway with heavy sheet steel had similarly actuated a steel window barrier.

With both door and window barred to exit, Doc drove his metallic fist against the plaster of the wall. It was a futile move. He found that the walls had been reënforced with heavy metal back of the plaster.

Still holding his breath against the anæsthetic vapor, Doc hurled himself across the room. He had one last hope—the movable panel in the roll-top desk. There was not time to look for the control key which would open the panel. There was time only to crash it in. Swiftly, Doc felt out the boundaries of the stout oak with his sensitive fingers.

Then his fists drummed a mighty tattoo. Fists were not enough. His shoulders lunged. He braced himself against the wall and kicked. His hand drifted out and contacted a heavy chair, swung it in a wide arc. The chair splintered in a dozen places, and the panel remained unmoved.

Doc was trapped! Not from the gas, however. That would become harmless in a few seconds, as it mingled more completely with the air.

Faintly, from an unidentifiable source, voices sounded. The words were not articulate, but Doc could recognize the tones. It was Renny and Long Tom shouting from some part of the building. They had heard the noise and, aware of Doc's presence in the building, they were shouting in the frantic hope that their voices might direct him to their rescue.

They had no way of knowing that the bronze man's situation was as desperate as their own.

Doc could breathe now. The anæsthetic gas had dissipated its powers, due to chemical reaction with the oxygen in the air.

Doc flung himself upon the massive roll-top desk. His attack was not chaotic, but planned so that he could use every muscle in his powerful body. Wedging himself on top of the writing surface with knees jackknifed in air, feet braced against one end, shoulders against the other, he pushed.

MUSCLES bunched and quivered, and suddenly his jackknifed knees went straight. There was a screeching of rent metal as he pried the desk apart. Doc parted the rest of the desk with his hands, making an opening large enough to squeeze through.

He found that the sliding panel had given onto a secret upward passage, converted from an old dumbwaiter shaft. Before plunging in, Doc leaped back into the room and examined the prone bodies of the two Asiatics.

He found about what he had expected. Both men were senseless from the anæsthetic gas and would remain so for some time.

Turning, Doc bolted for the dumbwaiter shaft. His hands closed on the rungs of a built-in ladder. He streaked upward like an islander climbing a palm.

A partition had been roofed across the shaft at the next floor level. In the side wall in front of him, Doc's probing fingers found a wooden door. His fists battered, the blows ringing hollowly. The door was as stout as the one built into the roll-top desk. It did not yield.

But Doc's pounding occasioned an uproar from the other side of the door. Voices came through in wild clamor.

"Doc, is it you——" That was Long Tom.

"Holy cow, Doc!" That would be Renny.

"Stand back from this door," Doc called.

He jackknifed his body between the door and the opposite shaft wall, using the same kind of bodily leverage he had utilized on the roll-top desk. The door broke in with splintering crash, and Doc was catapulted inside the room.

Beyond the Palisades, the sun had gone down. Already Broadway was blazing under a sun of its own making. A billion electric bulbs supplied scattered illumination for the rest of the city. But the room in which Doc stood reunited with Renny and Long Tom was dark. Electrical connections had long since been cut off from the outside.

Renny boomed, "The little squirt with the bush on his map yelled at us just before you came. He said——"

"——he's firing the building and leaving us to burn!" Long Tom cut in.

"This trap would go up like a gasoline tank, Doc."

Long Tom added, "We've been trying to break down the door——"

Renny cracked his big fists together, wailed, "I've nearly wore 'em out on that door, Doc! She almost breaks, but not quite."

It was evident to Doc that Renny considered his reputation at stake, as well as his life. Renny had long boasted—and backed up his boast—that his bare fists could pound the panel out of any wooden door.

"I smell smoke!" Long Tom gasped.

Doc's sensitive nostrils had already detected the acrid odor of the smoke.

"This building has been fired," he admitted.

"Listen!" Long Tom breathed.

A heart-stopping sound—the seething crackle of flames feeding through dry wooden floors, wafted to them faintly.

"We got to get out of here!" Renny blared.

"Right," Long Tom seconded.

"Come on, Renny," Doc directed. "We will try the door."

UNDER the combined fist battering and shoulder lunging of Doc and Renny, the door shuddered, groaned, then collapsed like a hut in a tornado. Smoke billowed in as all three men burst out. It was slightly lighter in the hall, in spite of the smoke.

"Stay close," Doc rapped, and leaped for the stairway.

Renny roared. "Holy cow! That's the wrong way!"

"The other way is down," Long Tom added.

Doc, taking the steps several at a time, did not pause to explain. He disappeared in the smoke and darkness of the floor above and forged on up the next flight of stairs. His flake-gold eyes, ever alert, had seen something his aids had missed.

Doc had glimpsed Boris Ramadanoff scuttling around the bend of the stair landing above. The bronze man's giant strides slashed the distance between himself and the murderous little man. At the top of the roof flight, Doc was only a little behind.

Ramadanoff went out on the roof like an eel. He got the door shut behind him. A snap lock caught and held as Doc rammed the panel with terrific force.

After Doc had tried his strength on the door that once, he did not waste time on it again.

From the roof, Boris Ramadanoff shouted with raw gloating: "Stay there and burn!"

Doc did not hear. He had already vaulted the bannister and landed on the smoke-filled floor below. He met Renny and Long Tom coming up.

"Down," he ordered. "Back into the room out of which we just came!"

"We can't, Doc!" Renny thumped.

"Fire's already cut us off from that floor!" Long Tom cried.

Creating its own draft, the fire funneled up the stairway below them. A few flights down, there was a crash as something collapsed.

"Down!" Doc ordered, and led the way.

Unquestioning, Long Tom and Renny followed him, shielding their eyes, slapping at flames that caught their clothes.

"This was our only chance," Doc threw out, as they gained the room.

Long Tom's eyes were seared shut with smoke. "Doc, where are you?"

"This way!"

They followed his voice, crowding into the shaft out of which Doc had smashed his way a few minutes before to rescue them. Splintering wood showered down on their heads.

"The building's falling!" Renny roared.

BUT it was only part of the building—the overhead partition which had been built in to seal off the shaftway. Doc had torn it out.

Doc said, "Follow me up. There's no ladder above. We will have to brace ourselves, feet and shoulders in the shaft, and shove with our hands. It is only two floors to the roof."

"Is the shaft open at the roof?" Long Tom gasped.

"If it is not, we will have to open it," Doc replied.

"What good's it gonna do to get on the roof?" Renny questioned, hoarsely.

"Save your breath," Doc advised. "Climb."

The shaft was not open at the roof. While the fire roared and crackled behind them, and smoke packed about them like black mortar, Doc struck and heaved against the roof surface which capped the shaftway.

The bronze man's metallic muscles were more enduring than the planks which opposed them. His prodigious hands tore out a hole big enough for his body to follow.

From the roof, a throbbing drone reached his ears. It was Boris Ramadanoff's gyro plane. It had taken Ramadanoff a few minutes to clear the airplane of its silk-cloth covering. But now the machine, its "windmill" revolving, was wrenched along by the navy-type catapult for a take-off.

The gyro pitched dangerously to one side, as it cleared the catapult. The side pitch gave Boris Ramadanoff a nasty moment, as the roof tops below tilted dizzily. But the whirling "windmill" blades steadied the plane, and Ramadanoff snatched an easy breath.

He was totally unaware of the reason for that unexpected side pitch.

Many curious persons, crowding the street to watch the fire, could have told him the cause. Gasps left many throats as watchers saw something they could hardly believe. They saw the gyro float up from the roof, glinting red in the lurid, reflected light of flames. That alone was exciting enough. An escape by airplane from a burning building!

The gasps which sprang from a multitude of lips, however, was not occasioned alone by the rising gyro. What brought the sound from throats was the figure of a man clinging to the tail skid of the gyro, causing the "windmill" plane to pitch alarmingly and the man's dangling body to swing from side to side.

The spectacle was visible for only an unreal instant. Then the lifting gyro and the man dangling in thin air from the understructure were blotted out by smoke.

If the awed watchers could have seen what followed they would have received an even greater thrill. Climbing with an agility made possible only by tremendous muscles, Doc worked astride the fuselage and toward the open cockpit of the gyro.

Boris Ramadanoff uttered a hoarse yell when, warned by the behavior of the plane, he turned and saw the bronze man come into view. The presence of Doc on the plane after an iron door had slammed in his face, locking him in a burning building, smacked momentarily of the supernatural—at least, to Ramadanoff. The bearded man, as though bitten by demons, reared up and plunged overboard from the opposite side of the cockpit.

His body dropped. He wore a parachute and this promptly bloomed, snubbing his fall.

Doc reached the cockpit and took the controls. Back to

the burning building, he headed. The crowd in the streets got another thrill. They saw the gyro float in through smoke, blood-red in the reflections of the flame, and like a gigantic humming bird, settle out of sight on the roof top.

The excitement the street watchers experienced was not a fraction of the one Long Tom and Renny felt, there on the blistering roof.

The crowd yelled itself hoarse when the gyro arose again. Most of them thought they were witnessing a sensational fire-department rescue, although a few noisily expressed the opinion that the whole thing was a publicity stunt of some kind.

Chapter X

EQUATORIAL FLIGHT

WHEN Boris Ramadanoff bailed out of the gyro, his parachute lowered him into a narrow strip of parkway between Riverside Drive and the Hudson River. There was but one person to witness his landing, that individual being a bench derelict, sodden with alcohol. He merely stared, wild-eyed, believing the spectacle of the man crashing into the underbrush with something like a bed sheet fluttering over his head to be a variation of the old "pink elephant" theme.

Boris Ramadanoff, therefore, was enabled to land virtually unseen. Skinning out of his 'chute harness and scrambling through the park shrubbery, he scurried up the long flight of stone steps to the street level and caught a taxi on the Drive. On Tenth Avenue, directly west of the Times Square district, he directed the driver to the curb.

"Wait for me," he called, and leaped out and ducked into a grimy doorway.

He was back soon, clutching a stiff object wrapped inside a trailing blanket.

"West Street!" he barked.

Riding toward the river, Ramadanoff took the ends of the blanket and wrapped them more snugly about the object which he carried.

West Street skirts the Hudson River and is lined with docks. When Ramadanoff let his taxi go, he walked a block down the dimly lit river-front street till he came to a large, roofed-over pier.

The huge, brick building, was smoke-stained, old-looking. There was nothing to distinguish it in appearance from any of a thousand other piers in New York, accommodating the world's shipping.

A sign over the corrugated metal door read:

HIDALGO TRADING COMPANY

As Ramadanoff very well knew, there *was* something unusual about this pier. It was not, practically speaking, a pier at all. It was Doc Savage's water-front hangar. It housed an assortment of heavier-than-air craft as remarkable as the ultra-modern land vehicles garaged in the basement of Doc's skyscraper headquarters.

Ramadanoff made no attempt to force an entrance into the sprawling bulk of the hangar. He had scouted the locale before. He knew that the hangar, protected by photo-electric eyes and magnetic fields, was as impossible of entrance as a bank vault would have been.

What he did was ridiculously simple. On each side of the driveway door was head-high, rather scrawny, shrubbery. Ramadanoff moved along the dim street until his dark figure merged with the shadows of the shrubbery.

Any one watching could have observed that his figure did not show again on the other side of the shrubbery. But there was no one watching. The little man squirmed into the very center of the concealing branches and crouched down. He pulled the blanket wrapping from his parcel, exposing a sub-machine gun of non-glinting blue-metal finish.

WHEN Ramadanoff, weaponless, had ducked out of the taxi into the Tenth Avenue doorway, it was to make a lightning quick call on one of Jans Bergman's men who had a room at the address. Bergman's demise was not yet known to his men, so it had been no trouble for Ramadanoff to arrange for the use of the machine gun.

Doc Savage, Ramadanoff knew, would waste no time in arriving at the hangar to take off for the Galapagos. Of course, Doc would go by plane.

But the bronze man, Ramadanoff was determined, would never even enter that hangar. He would drop before a withering blast of ambush lead.

After a while, a sedan rolled down the street and nosed silently in the Hidalgo Trading Company's driveway.

Ramadanoff's pulse quickened, then slowed. He had expected Doc to stop the car and get out and open the hangar door. But the car ran on without slackening of speed, pointing head-on for the closed roll-down door. At the instant Ramadanoff expected a collision, the door rolled silently upward, actuated by a short-wave radio beam transmitted from within the car to a detector-relay device connected to an electric door-opening mechanism.

Doc's car disappeared within the hangar and the door closed down.

Ramadanoff's face was purpled from his rage at missing the last chance he would have to prevent Doc from flying to the island. He had a ferocious impulse to empty the machine-gun drum against the corrugated metal door in sheer insane frustration.

A moment later, he was glad that he had not wasted those bullets. Amazingly, the door opened again.

Ramadanoff could hear a scuffling of shoe leather against dusty concrete. Then a huge bronze figure became visible in the door.

The drowsy quiet of early evening was smashed by thunderous, macabre rattle as Ramadanoff held the trigger and swung his stream of leaden death back and forth. Mindful of bullet-proof garments, he aimed high, for the face. A great many bullets sprayed harmlessly against the corrugated metal surface of the hangar front.

But fully a score were direct face hits on the bronze man's figure in the doorway.

There might have been more hits; but suddenly the machine gun silenced. A crashing weight had descended into the shrubbery, apparently from the clouds, grinding the underbrush, the assassin, and the machine gun into the ground. Ramadanoff's finger was broken before he could clear it from the trigger. But the finger was the least of his troubles. He felt himself lifted and slammed. He knew what had him. Doc Savage!

Doc had leaped from a hidden door high in the warehouse side, directly on top of Ramadanoff. Doc dragged Ramadanoff inside the hangar door and said to Long Tom, "Haul Robbie in and get the door shut."

Long Tom chuckled. "Robbie will be needin' a new paint job on his face, Doc."

"Yeah," Renny boomed. "And a set of new teeth."

Ramadanoff stared, bleary-eyed, as Long Tom and Renny pushed the huge bronze figure, which had appeared in the doorway and taken the bullets, inside, and closed the hangar door.

"A dummy!" he ejaculated.

"Sure," Long Tom said. "A mechanical likeness of Doc. Robbie, the Robot."

"And can Robbie take it?" Renny rumbled.

"Had his face shot off him four times, so far," Long Tom added.

Ramadanoff was muttering profanely to himself.

"Don't you get it, Whiskers?" Long Tom demanded.

Ramadanoff scowled.

Renny explained sardonically: "Doc likes to coöperate, so he provided the shrubbery outside for guys that want to pot him from cover. Doc ordered the bushes big, so as to give plenty of room for a man with a gun to hide inside."

Long Tom continued, "And the bushes are wired so that any one crowding inside of 'em will cause a signal to flash."

Doc was already penetrating deep within the hangar.

"Come on," he called back.

Dragging their prisoner, Renny and Long Tom hurried after Doc Savage.

The bronze man was swinging inside the cabin of his large speed ship, a three-motor job with streamlined alloy hull. The wings tapered into the fuselage for minimum wind resistance. It was a combination land-and-sea plane and had a speed of nearly three hundred miles an hour.

"We taking this one, Doc?" Long Tom queried, hand waving out to indicate the plane before them.

"Right," the bronze man said.

Renny and Long Tom shoved their prisoner inside and piled in after him.

WITH the three supercharged motors delivering their full quota of power, the big speed plane hurtled south through the Atlantic seaboard darkness.

They caught the slumberous twinkle of early morning lights in Cuba and roared on, doing better than three hundred miles an hour as they climbed high and rode the stratospheric air currents to the Canal Zone.

At Colon, they got a surprise.

They set down for refueling. A dark-skinned man in a white linen suit popped out of the directional radio station operated by the department of commerce and ran across the field toward Doc's plane. The man was waving a radiogram.

"For Doc Savage," he called.

The dark-skinned man leaned against the low-slung cabin with a hand resting on the ledge of an opened porthole, and his black eyes were centered in rapt admiration on Doc as the bronze giant opened the envelope and read the radiogram.

HAVE DISCOVERED BORIS RAMADANOFF IS
WORKING WITH HIS BROTHER COUNT RAMA-
DANOFF STOP DISREGARD OUR OTHER RADIO-
GRAM STOP ALIVE BUT MAY NOT BE FOR
LONG STOP BETTER DO THINGS

MONK

Doc handed the radiogram to his aids.

"Huh!" Renny snorted. "We got Boris's number before
they did, I guess."

"They're still alive," Long Tom said, tensely.

"Yeah, and we'll be there in a few hours," Renny
thumped.

"Watch the plane," Doc instructed Renny. "Do not let
Ramadanoff out, or let anybody else come near."

Doc, with Long Tom, the electrical wizard, accompanied
the dark-skinned man back to the broadcasting station to
try to get a line on what was the matter with the radio
beam.

"A ship carrying one of my aids, while following your
beam, was recently thrown off its course and wrecked," Doc
advised.

"The trouble must have been with the receiving apparatus,"
the dark-skinned man said.

"Impossible!" interposed Long Tom, who had made the
boat's radio installation and knew it was as perfect as was
possible.

"Then examine my layout," the radio station attendant
invited.

Doc and Long Tom made a careful examination, then returned to the plane.

"What'd you find out over there?" Renny queried.

Long Tom answered, "Everything was in perfect mechanical
shape."

Refueled, the plane took off, soared high over the feverish
Panama jungle, then left the lush green for the sparkling
blue of the Pacific as, engines throbbing, it bored steadily
southward toward the Galapagos.

Long Tom was bending over the audio-frequency amplifier. He jerked his head phones off and held one to Doc's
ear. A dot-dash combination in sharp staccato sounded
plainly.

"The A wave is coming in too strongly," Long Tom said.

"Are we off the course?" Renny rumbled.

"We are off the course as transmitted by the beam an-
tenna back at the Canal Zone," Doc stated.

"But that's the right course," Renny protested.

"Is it?" Doc asked mildly.

"IT's the beam the others were riding when their ship piled on the rocks," Renny rumbled. "We want to go where they were wrecked, don't we?"

"Yes," Doc said. "But this beam may not be directing us there."

"I get it," Renny muttered. "If there's nothing the matter with the instruments, the trouble must lie with that dark-skinned baby at the Canal Zone who is transmitting the signals."

Doc nodded. "He transmitted the beam so that it put Johnny on the rocks. It may be that now he is laying down a beam which, if we follow it, will land us in the Pacific Ocean with empty gas tanks."

Renny snorted, "Thinks he's sendin' us on a one-way trip, huh?"

Long Tom was struck with an idea. "Stop me, if you've thought of this one, Doc—but how does the course, as broadcast to us by the radio beacon, compare with the latitude and longitude of the island as given you by Boris Ramadanoff?"

"The two check perfectly," Doc said.

"Then Ramadanoff gave us the wrong directions, too?"

"It is almost certain that he did."

"Want me to bring him in, Doc?" Renny asked, eagerly.

"Yes," Doc said. "It is time Ramadanoff talked."

Renny hurried aft, unlocked a small individual cabin, roused Boris Ramadanoff out and trundled him forward to Doc. The bronze man turned the plane controls over to the sensitive mechanical arms of a robot pilot, and faced Boris Ramadanoff.

"I want the latitude and longitude of your brother's island," Doc announced.

"I gave it to you——"

"I want the correct latitude and longitude," Doc interrupted, severely.

"The one I gave you is correct," the little man insisted, stubbornly.

Doc fixed his gold-flecked eyes on Ramadanoff while he spoke in brittle tones to Renny and Long Tom.

"Get out the rope, Renny, and loop it over Ramadanoff's right foot," the bronze man said. "Long Tom, open the side hatch."

Renny looped the rope over Ramadanoff's foot and pulled

it tight. Renny hauled back so exuberantly that he pulled the bearded little man off his feet. Long Tom threw open the side hatch, revealing a patch of blue—the Pacific Ocean— perhaps a mile below.

"Pull his 'chute off, Long Tom," Doc directed.

Long Tom slipped the pack-'chute from the little man's shoulders. The packs, contrivances developed by Doc himself, were not bulky, and they could be worn with no more inconvenience than a heavy coat would have occasioned. Doc and his men, when in the air, were usually equipped with the safety devices, and, in this case, they had provided one for their prisoner.

Doc looked at Ramadanoff, and said, "Renny, here, is going to lower you through the hole. He will lower you down hand over hand, slowly, till he comes to the end of the rope. Then, if you have not indicated that you will speak the truth, he will let go the rope."

Doc looked toward Renny. "Lower away."

Ramadanoff had been lowered half of the rope's length when the bluff worked. He looked up and squalled like a wild cat.

"I'll tell!" he screamed.

"Hold him there a minute, Renny," Doc ordered. He looked down at the cringing prisoner. "The location?"

Ramadanoff screamed latitude and longitude down to minutes and seconds. He had it on the tip of his tongue.

"WE will let him cool off now," Doc decided. "Renny, take charge of him."

"Will I, Doc!" Renny boomed.

Ramadanoff was so giddy from being dangled on the rope that he could not stand when he was first drawn back within the plane. Long Tom fitted the pack-'chute back on the man's shoulders, and Renny dragged him ungently aft and locked him in the fuselage compartment again.

The plane ran into a fog bank as it droned southwest. Doc climbed the plane and came out on top, in dazzling sunshine. Occasional rifts in the fog showed him the blue Pacific below.

Eventually, a rent showed something else besides water.

"Land below," Renny announced. "A small island."

"Cocos Island," Doc said. "We take our final bearings from here. The next land we sight will be the Galapagos."

"That won't be long, at the rate we're traveling," Long Tom said.

It was only a brief glimpse they got of Cocos Island, then

the fog closed in again like swaddling cotton, seeming to wedge the hurtling plane against the sky.

"Bring out the prisoner, Renny," Doc suggested, some time later. "We will try again to find out something more about this mysterious Devil's Honeycomb."

Renny grinned, and went aft to unlock the compartment door.

"We'll make him talk," Long Tom affirmed, grimly.

But they did not make Boris Ramadanoff talk.

Renny threw open the prison compartment door and stared, jaw sagging, his generously proportioned mouth yawning wide like a tunnel opening.

"What's the matter?" Long Tom called, sharply.

"Matter!" Renny howled, dazedly. He turned, dived forward.

"He busted a hole in the floor!" Renny squalled. "He's jumped out!"

"How could he break out?" Long Tom demanded. "Nobody can break through the alloy skin of this plane. It's even bulletproof."

"How did he do it, Renny?" Doc asked, quietly.

"That was the compartment where we had the floor ripped up the other day, Doc," Renny muttered. "It wasn't welded; just small bolts set in temporarily."

Doc looked at the chart. "It is too late to do anything about it now. Doubtless, Ramadanoff bailed out over Cocos Island. It is entirely too large an island for us to waste time trying to locate him."

The great tri-motored speed ship scudded on, riding above the fog bank like a gigantic water bug skimming the surface of quiet depths.

"How're we gonna locate anything in this fog?" Renny wanted to know, later.

"We can get our latitude and longitude above, then go down and land on the water to wait till the fog lifts," Doc explained. "That, of course, may not be necessary."

That logical plan, it developed later, was never to be put into execution. At the present latitude and longitude, given by Boris Ramadanoff under pressure, the fog became strangely reddish in color over a considerable area. This crimson glow was uneasy, flickering, brightening and dulling as though the leaping fires of hell itself strove to break through.

Doc banked the speed plane in a wide spiral around the scarlet-stained sector.

"What caused that?" Renny rumbled, awe making his voice somehow queer.

"Volcano," Doc decided. "Active."

"Let's ease down," Long Tom suggested.

They did go down, but not easily.

An ear-splitting crash sent a convulsion through the plane, then tilted it in a mad dip. Accompanying the detonation, flame sheeted out, enveloping them. They were stunned, temporarily blinded.

"Whole back end blown off!" Renny bawled.

"Lost half the fuselage!" Long Tom shouted.

The plane was plummeting, weaving dizzily, shuddering and bouncing in the air as against something solid.

"Jump!" Doc ordered. "Spill air to guide your 'chutes away from the red portion of the fog!"

Chapter XI

SHREDDED DEATH

THE plane had been very high when the explosion occurred. Their parachutes were larger than the average, so they went down slowly; and because they pulled at shrouds on one side, they skidded through the sky. They left the domain of lurid red light behind.

In fact, lost from everything but each other in the fog, they overdid the skidding a little. They came down in water.

Close over the sea, the fog was thin. Doc and Renny, releasing themselves from the parachute harnesses a few feet above the water, plunged into the seething gray expanse within easy hailing distance of each other. Long Tom plummeted down farther to the left; where the plane hit, they could not tell, although it was probably nearer shore and off to the left.

Treading water and trying to orient himself in the smother of waves, Renny bawled, "What caused that explosion, Doc?"

"A bomb, obviously," the bronze man shouted back.

"But we searched Ramadanoff before we brought him aboard," Renny pointed out.

"Ramadanoff did not do it," Doc returned. "It must have been done at the Canal Zone landing field——"

"The dark-skinned guy!" Renny roared. "The one who brought the radiogram out—and stood by while we read it!"

"Right," Doc agreed. "The fellow evidently had his orders in advance."

Renny took water, coughed it up and sputtered, "But what made the thing go off right when we were over the island?"

"Probably a radio control detonator, actuated by a transmitter below," Doc Savage hazarded. "The mechanism would have been fairly simple for a good radio technician to construct."

The bronze man was treading water. The water all about them seemed to be swirling, like a furiously running stream. There was a pronounced undercurrent that at times nearly took them under.

"Holy cow!" Renny thumped. "Some swimming pool!"

"A tide rip," Doc Savage offered. "It seems to be carrying us offshore."

Unexpectedly, a streak of phosphorescence angled in toward the bronze man. The streak was preceded by a water-slashing fin.

"Sharks!" Long Tom yelled from near by.

But Doc had already seen the racing black fin.

"Make for the reef!" the bronze man shouted to Long Tom.

The black fin, swerving close to Doc, went under in a boil of bubbles and phosphorescence. Doc went under, too. Half a minute later, Long Tom uttered a hoarse cry and kicked out with his feet. He thought he was being attacked by the shark; but it was only Doc, who had swum under water and come up alongside him.

With Doc's assistance, Long Tom gained rapidly in his fight against the current. Nearing the coral reef and temporary safety, a shark slashed in at them.

"Try to make it alone," Doc jerked, and disappeared under water again, almost under the chisel nose of the attacking shark. The shark dove with the bronze man, rolling.

Long Tom made it to the jagged reef, and a moment later Doc stroked up and muscled out of the water alongside him.

LONG TOM coughed water. "Playing tag with that man-eater—drawing him away—you saved my life, Doc——"

"Listen," Doc cautioned.

The *put-put* of a motor launch sounded strongly.

"What'll we do?" Long Tom gulped.

"Could you make it ashore, swimming?"

"Afraid not," Long Tom puffed. "I was almost gone when you reached me."

"Renny might not make it either," Doc said, thoughtfully.

The motor launch nosed around a wave-laced reef into close view. Men in the bucking launch waved. Doc answered their signals.

Long Tom growled tragically, "Wrecked just when we could begin to do some good! Our superfirers, all our weapons, at the bottom of the ocean! And now we'll be taken prisoners the same as Johnny, Pat, Monk, Ham and the rest of 'em."

A bellow of distress reached them faintly through the whipping wind.

"It's Renny!" Long Tom gasped. "Sharks!"

Doc took the water in a shallow dive which bounced him to the surface and sent him streaking through the short, steep waves toward Renny's voice.

The motor launch came on, picked up Long Tom and bore down upon Doc and Renny. A boat hook snagged Renny's collar and drew him alongside. Hands reached down and helped him aboard.

"Sharks!" some one exploded. "Right alongside!"

A boat hook probed at Doc. The shark reached the bronze man. Doc and the shark disappeared in a welter of churning water. Bubbles streamed up and broke whitely on the dark surface.

But only at first did they break whitely. Very soon, they were breaking red. The red stain spread over the water, a gory blanket around the pitching launch.

Renny and Long Tom stared at the water in dawning horror. The half dozen men who had come out in the launch crowded the rails, chattering in queer languages as they scanned the surface looking for visual evidence of the tragedy indicated as occurring below.

Blood in the water brought more sharks closing in. The launch threaded back and forth until the red stain was diffused; but Doc did not again appear.

The helmsman swung the launch around and started bucking the currents toward the shore.

All the crew were dressed in the same fashion—simple loin cloths, and collars of lizard hide. The launch docked at a pier running out from the palace of the Ramadanoffs.

Inside the palace, in the huge room—that high-vaulted cavern fashioned from wooden beams and black volcanic rock—Long Tom and Renny were welcomed by the Count Ramadanoff in the same suavely polite manner in which he had greeted Monk, Ham and Pat.

The heatless blue flames leaped as before within the mammoth fireplace, causing shadows to dart and vanish throughout the luxuriantly furnished hall. From high overhead, the crystal-spangled candelabra, hanging from its massive chain and burning fully two hundred candles, shed a yellow light which penetrated weirdly to the middle stair landing hung with the long curtains of somber ruby velvet.

Long Tom and Renny, grief-torn as they were by Doc's

disappearance after the attack by the shark, could not help but feel the menace which stalked through the dank air of the place.

The Count Ramadanoff, himself, appeared as some one not quite real. He was a towering giant, almost as large as Doc—this much they realized. With his Czar-of-Russia beard, his courtly bearing, he appeared to be a replica of his brother, Boris—a replica fully twice as large.

The count bowed, said precisely: "My guests have a predilection for arriving here in wet clothes. I will have a change of dry garments laid out for you."

The count's thin lips writhed back to emit a sharp cobra-like hissing. A wizened slave padded forward on bare feet in answer to the summons.

While the count issued orders for the preparation of a chamber for his guests, Long Tom murmured an aside to Renny: "You see what I do?"

Renny grunted. "The slave! He's a member of Johnny's expedition—or was, wasn't he?"

Long Tom nodded. "We've got to put on an act, until we get the lay of things here. It's all queer."

"And we can't let this whiskered devil know we think Doc is dead," Renny whispered.

The count looked sharply at Renny.

"So," he murmured, "the bronze man is dead!"

Renny stared belligerently, aware that the count must have read his lips.

Long Tom smoothed things over. While Renny's big fists started swinging nervously at his sides, Long Tom said, "There seems to be a mistake. It's the shark that's dead."

The count's eyes glittered. "I hope you are right. I am eager to meet personally this Doc Savage."

"What we want to know," Renny put in bluntly, "is where are Ham, Monk, Johnny and Pat?"

The count answered precisely: "You have reference, doubtless, to Brigadier General Theodore Marley Brooks, Lieutenant Colonel Andrew——"

"Yeah," Renny interrupted, "they're the ones! Where are they?"

The count shrugged. "How should I know? This is an extremely remote island in the Galapagos, not an information booth."

Renny's glance roved fiercely around the great hall and fastened for an instant upon the grand piano draped with rich sea-otter furs.

The count's cruel eyes flashed. "I assure you, my dear

Renwick, the persons you mentioned are not concealed in my piano."

The slave in his loin cloth and lizard-hide collar, padded down the broad stone steps and prostrated himself before his master. But his eyes, for a flashing instant, had caught Long Tom's with a significant glance.

"You may follow the slave," the count announced. "When you have changed to dry clothing, I will receive you down here."

As Long Tom and Renny mounted the sweeping spiral of the stairs and passed beyond the ruby-colored drape held back by the slave, Count Ramadanoff's voice followed them with suave menace.

"One thing, remember," Ramadanoff intoned: "The shadow of the Devil's Honeycomb lies everywhere upon this island."

INSIDE the chamber assigned them, the slave bent to take off Long Tom's wet shoes. Renny reached down and poked a huge thumb and finger under the man's chin and tilted his head up.

"Don't you know us?" he asked.

The man squirmed, looking at Renny out of fear-haunted eyes.

"Not I," he whispered. "I don't know you."

"Downstairs, you did," Long Tom suggested.

"That was before he reminded me."

"Reminded you of what?"

The man's voice rasped hoarsely. "That the Devil's Honeycomb is a menace everywhere on the island!"

"Where's the rest of your party?" Renny demanded.

"I don't know anything!" the man mumbled.

"You mean you won't talk."

The man's lips whitened. "Anybody who tells anything on this island dies!"

Renny grunted with disgust at the display of fear.

"It ought to be safe to talk here," Long Tom urged.

"It's safe nowhere," muttered the other. "You talk and you die."

"How do you know?" the electrical wizard insisted.

"Mister, I've been standin' close when it happened," the slave mumbled. "A little hole comes in your temple, about the size you could jab your thumb into."

"Baloney," Renny summed it up.

Suddenly flooding the room, a weird, strumming music vibrated. Fantastic melody! It struck the ear with pulsations that seemed to raise goose flesh over the entire body and cause the hair to tug at its roots.

"What's that?" Renny demanded, glaring about, swinging his big fists.

The man who had become a slave was staring with panic-bulged eyes. He choked out words, "The count playin' at the piano!"

"So what?" Renny boomed.

"So somebody dies!"

"Nuts!" Renny rumbled.

The man rasped stubbornly, "Every time I've heard him play like that, somebody has died right after! Why, your own men, and the girl——" He choked off his words with spasmodic effort.

Both Long Tom and Renny seized him and shook him simultaneously.

"What about our men and the girl?" Renny's great voice was thunder.

In the grand hall below, the music had stopped, though faint mocking echoes hung about like an exotic perfume.

"All right!" the man gasped. "I'll tell you! I might die for it; but if I don't tell you I'll die anyway. But first, is it true that Doc Savage is dead?"

"A shark took Doc," Renny said, bleakly. "He didn't come up."

The man wilted. "Then it's no use! Without Savage we can't——"

"Talk!" Long Tom jabbed. "What were you going to tell us?"

The man opened his mouth to speak. But it was not his voice which Long Tom and Renny heard. There was a flesh-crawling sound—a bony crunch, and the man who would have talked plunged forward, his head striking solidly on the floor, his body flopping over and lying inert.

RENNY and Long Tom stared wildly. There had been no visible movement within the room—just that crunch, then the man falling limply.

Renny, fists swinging, went tearing around the room, pulling aside curtains, banging closet doors, looking under the beds.

He found nothing.

With Long Tom, he examined the limp body. The man was dead from a wound in his temple, a hole a bird's egg might have dropped into—or a man's thumb.

All at once, welling with chill mockery, music from the count's piano flowed through the room again.

Renny jerked upright, swerved for the door.

"Come on!" he barked at Long Tom.

"Come on where?"

"To punch the count's face out from between his pointed ears!" Renny roared. "We'll settle all this mystery now!"

"It's a good idea," Long Tom agreed, and plunged out after Renny.

Past the hanging ruby drapes on the middle landing and down the wide stone steps, three at a time, they rushed. The count rose from his piano to confront them with suave dignity.

"Why do you hurry, gentlemen?" he questioned, dark eyebrows arched.

Momentarily disarmed by the count's quiet manner, they slowed their precipitous descent, came forward slowly.

"But you have still your wet clothes on, gentlemen!" the count chided.

"When we get through, you won't worry about clothes!" Renny threatened.

"Who killed the man in our room?" Long Tom demanded.

The count smiled thinly. "Your bellicose manner becomes understandable. A man has been killed, you say?"

"In our room!" Long Tom grated.

The big bearded man queried, "There is, perhaps, a hole in his temple?"

"If you know that, you did it!" Renny howled, starting his forward rush.

The count, unperturbed, lifted a hand. "One moment, my dear Renwick. It is only natural that I should know about the thumb-hole death. Such deaths occur with great frequency on this island."

While he talked, the count's white, tapering fingers toyed with a small object—a slim thing of flashing gold.

Long Tom moved forward to look at the gold thing.

"Pat Savage's lipstick!" he clipped, horrified.

Long Tom's hand reached out. "Let me see that."

"With pleasure." The count handed over the lipstick.

"It *is* Pat's!" Long Tom muttered, examining it. He glared at the count. "Where'd you get it? You said you hadn't seen Pat. Where is she? Snappy, brother, before we give you what is known as the works!"

"Ridiculous!" the count asserted. "In your United States, lipsticks are mass-production articles. There must be upward of half a million of this identical design."

"There aren't half a million of *these!*" Renny's voice

sounded in a bawl of hoarse triumph, as he rushed to a corner and seized a slim black malacca cane, held it up.

"Ham's sword cane!" Long Tom echoed.

Renny faced Count Ramadanoff. "Here's Ham's cane! I want to know where Ham is."

"You are making yourself utterly ridiculous," the count asserted.

"Brother, you asked for it!" Renny roared, and rushed the count, striking out with his great fists.

The count made no attempt to dodge. He stood and took it—and in return laid his fist against Renny's jaw in a blow which rocked the big engineer back on his heels.

Renny blinked dazedly. He had never met opposition like this in his life. He could almost believe that it was Doc Savage's powerful muscles that had just put those staggering blows across.

Long Tom was helpless to aid, because, at a nod from the count, a slave—a squat Mongol—had appeared from behind a wall drape and nudged Long Tom's ribs with the flare-lipped muzzle of a diabolical poison dart gun.

Renny tried everything—science, brute force, but he might as well have been fighting a shadow, for all the impression he made.

Finally, the count grew weary of the sport. Eyes glinting, thin lips drawn back to a thin line, he put over a haymaker. Then he stood over Renny, callously kicking him back to consciousness.

"I will always regret that I did not meet your Doc Savage," the count said gloatingly, and sighed. "It appears that I must live all my life without meeting a foe worthy of my efforts."

He hissed again and the slaves bound and dragged the two prisoners out of the main hall and part way up the tower steps. Before the same slot in the tower hall which Doc's other aids had been forced to look through, Renny and Long Tom were halted.

"Observe your playmates," the count directed.

THEY looked through the slot, and in that courtyard dungeon, hemmed in by starkly rearing palace walls, they saw the same unbelievable monster that Monk, Ham and Pat had witnessed.

"Holy cow!" Renny breathed.

Squatting in the middle of the flagstoned pit, bathed in the red volcanic glare, was a creature that had a ridge of toothlike horns running down his scabrous back and tail.

Swinging its armored head upward, it snorted two streams of vapor from its nostrils; then it drew in air, and its sides swelled out until, to the horrified glance of Renny and Long Tom, the loathsome thing threatened to expand to such a bulk that it would fill the whole courtyard.

"What is it?" Long Tom gulped.

"I don't know," Renny said, suddenly hoarse.

"In observing this Gargantuan monstrosity," the count's odious voice broke in, "do not overlook the cells under the balcony—your temporary abode. I say 'temporary' because the cell bars are movable, actuated electrically at my desire—my desire being dictated to a large extent by the humor of the creature you are observing."

Again the count sounded his ghoulish hiss, and Long Tom and Renny were hustled down the stairs, out onto the circular balcony which ran all the way around the courtyard dungeon and thrust unceremoniously through a trapdoor in the balcony floor. They landed heavily ten feet below on the flagstoned floor of a cell.

Through the heavy iron bars they could see clearly in the courtyard. The monster had retreated out of sight into its den.

Opposite them, on the balcony, the count looked down. "The creature has enjoyed itself for the day," he informed. "He will sleep before he needs diversion and exercise again."

Suddenly, Renny and Long Tom reached out and clutched each other, trembling. They had seen the same things almost at the same instant.

There, almost under their feet, were four shapeless, mauled bodies. The flags of the court were stained a ghastly red that did not come from the reflected volcanic light. Remnants of clothes clung to each torn body. And Long Tom and Renny were recognizing those remnants!

They were the claw-and-teeth-shredded garments of Johnny and Ham and Monk and Pat.

"And the shark got Doc Savage," the count remarked, looking down from his balcony.

Chapter XII

THE HONEYCOMB HORROR

THE Count Ramadanoff was somewhat mistaken.

The shark did *not* get Doc. The red smudge which had bloomed on the water was not occasioned by the shark's flat, pointed teeth tearing at the bronze man, but came from wounds inflicted by Doc's slashing knife on the shark itself.

After beating off the shark's attack, Doc swam under water and came up out of sight of the launch, behind a jutting coral reef. He waited until the boat had churned away through chopping waves, then struck out in the long, hard swim for the island.

Doc had touched shore on a lava-strewn beach, waded through a belt of brown sea weed, and plunged into the obscurity of shoreline vegetation—wind-bent trees bleached white with ocean spray, and dangling, cobra-headed Peruvian cactus.

Doc drove on through the thorn-studded undergrowth and came out on a broad, well-defined game trail. He recognized it as an age-old path used by the Galapagos tortoises as they butted through the jungle between their feeding grounds and watering places.

It was evening and the volcano was blinking its red light over the island when Doc reached the high plateau, pocked by those mysterious, man-made honeycomb pits. He forged forward, keeping to the jungle fringe until he arrived near the active workings.

From a cactus covert he watched, gold-flecked eyes weirdly alive, while the overseers strode up and down before the long line of pits and cracked their whips over the backs of the chained slaves digging their way to death from exhaustion in the strange honeycomb pattern of circular holes.

The bronze man watched for a chance to maneuver closer

and examine the pits. But, since the disturbance created by his aids on the day they had been wrecked on the island, the guards had been doubled. Doc had no opportunity to get close enough to look down.

AHEAD of the advancing line of pits, perhaps fifty yards distant on the high plateau floor, loomed a small stockade containing surplus working tools; it was guarded by four men, beefy-shouldered, swarthy fellows, their seminude bodies glistening with a hard burnish whenever the volcano lighted up the sky with its hellish red glare.

They talked among themselves in brittle Asiatic gibberish.

One of them clacked suddenly in his native tongue, "That flat rock out there, where did it come from?"

The volcanic fire died down before his companions could look.

"I remember no rock out there," one of them said.

"Then look the next time the glow comes," the other suggested.

Momentarily, the lurid lightning sheeted out again.

"Look!" the sharp-eyed one exploded.

"Look where?" the other snapped.

"I *am* looking," a third said. "I see nothing."

"Are you trying to fool us?" the fourth remarked. "There is nothing there."

"But before, there was a rock!" the first guard growled, stubbornly. "I am sure——"

In the blanketing darkness, the man's voice was cut off with a muffled gurgle.

"What's wrong with you?" a companion asked, sharply. "Did you swallow a bug——"

There was another muffled gurgle as this man ceased speaking in the same abrupt manner as the first.

Together the other two men clacked in alarm: "What is the matter——"

They never learned what it was. Two gurgles sounded simultaneously; and after that came silence. For, all evidence to the contrary, it might have been the equatorial darkness, pressing malignantly close, which had choked all four watchers into insensibility.

Volcanic light gleamed again over the honeycomb pattern of pits on the high plain. The light revealed the four guards sitting silently upright, their backs to the stockade —while inside the stockade a giant bronze man moved, selecting a digging instrument, a wedge-pointed pick.

The light went out, then flared again and revealed a lump

that might have been a bronze-hued rock on the plateau, halfway between the stockade and fringing underbrush. But the next time red light rippled out, the stone had vanished —and Doc Savage, under cover of the thorny bush, was creeping toward the line of pits with the wedge-pointed pick in his hand.

He had silenced the guards by deft pressure exerted on nerve centers at the back of their necks with his cabled fingers. It would be hours, perhaps, before the guards regained consciousness.

Doc passed by the front line of pits in which the chained slaves were digging, and watching his chance, crawled over and dropped inside one of the worked-out cells immediately behind the active front row.

Doc crouched with pick in hand and commenced rapidly digging a hole in the circular walls. The wall separating the cells was thin. In a matter of minutes, Doc had picked a hole large enough to let him look through.

It had been Doc's intention to contact one slave after another in this manner, until he came upon one who could furnish information regarding the fate of his aids. As he looked through the fist-sized hole he had dug, his trilling sounded faintly.

The chained slave heard, and stiffened visibly. This slave was an astounding individual, with a massive hairy torso, neck nearly as thick as his broad head and long, gorillalike arms extending almost to his knees. There was such strength in that hairy body that the man could bite his shovel into the flint-packed volcanic ash without the necessity of loosening it first with the pick.

The gory glow of volcanic light illuminated the man's face briefly, revealing a sprawled nose, a huge gash of mouth and a forehead almost buried in bristling hair. The man was so incredibly homely that he was rather pleasant to look at—like a genial bull-dog.

He kept digging, but his keen little eyes had detected the hole Doc had gouged in the pit wall. He heaved close, the chain rattling against his leg iron.

His voice was small, childish, jerky with emotion.

"Blazes, Doc! How'd you get here?"

"Give me the story, Monk," Doc whispered, guardedly.

"We're all alive—but we wouldn't be, much longer," Monk said, making his small voice smaller.

"The situation seemed desperate, from that second radiogram you sent to intercept me at the Canal Zone," Doc said. "Or did you send it, Monk?"

"We only sent one, Doc—to New York," Monk grunted.

"The second message sounded so legitimate that it deflected my attention enough for Count Ramadanoff's agent to get a time-bomb in our plane," Doc said, grimly; "which, of course, was why the radiogram was sent."

"Did you crash here, Doc?" Monk demanded.

"Offshore. Renny and Long Tom are prisoners. Where are the others?"

"Ham's chained in the pit next to me, and Johnny is in the one beyond that," Monk advised.

Doc breathed, "And Pat."

"As far as I know, the count's got her cooped up in his palace. We got to get her out. The count's got a man-eatin' beast there as big as a mountain. I know it doesn't sound sane, but all of us saw the thing. *Whew!*"

Doc asked, "You were imprisoned for a time at the palace?"

"Yeah, but when old bush-face saw how tough we were, he sent us here to kill ourselves diggin', instead of feedin' us to his critter," Monk growled. "That man-eatin' thing has even got teeth on its back, Doc! You wouldn't believe a monster like that was in the world!"

A GUARD passed by and looked down, lashed with his whip. A red welt sprang out on Monk's shoulder.

"Quit mumblin' to yourself," the guard directed in English. "And dig faster!"

After the guard continued on, Monk gritted through the hole to Doc, "You see how it is? Most of the diggers die off quick."

"Why the pits?" Doc queried.

"You've got me," Monk grunted. "We've sure wondered about 'em."

"I'm going to dig through into your pit, Monk," Doc informed. "Stand so your back will hide me as much as possible."

After Doc entered Monk's pit, he dug his way quickly through into Ham's. Monk filled both the holes as best he could. Doc, in the adjoining pit with Ham, kept close to the wall so that, unless one of the overseers stepped close and looked directly down, he would remain undetected.

Ham stifled his amazement at Doc's appearance; and Doc, reaching out with his pick, gouged an entrance for himself into Johnny's pit.

Almost the instant he arrived alongside Johnny, things began to happen.

"I'll be superamalgamated!" the bony geologist exploded, as Doc squirmed into view.

"Say it louder!" Doc directed.

"What?" Johnny blurted, startled.

"Say it louder," Doc repeated.

Johnny was so surprised at the whole business that he did not speak out in his accustomed verbose manner.

"It'll bring the guards down on us!" he protested.

"That," Doc said, "is what we want."

"I'll be superamalgamated!" Johnny blurted his favorite expression again.

"Louder!" the bronze man directed.

Johnny gulped, raised his voice with determination.

"I'll be superamalgamated, superagalmated, superaglerated —aw nuts, Doc, you say it!" The word, for once, had gotten him down.

But it was not necessary for Doc to say it. An overseer lunged toward the pit. Doc was back against the side. The overseer did not observe him. The whip cracked down at Johnny. Doc's hands reached out, grasped the slashing rawhides, gave a downward jerk.

The unexpected tug pulled the overseer off balance before he had time to brace himself or let go the whip. He teetered on the brink of the pit, then fell inward, sprawling. Doc's fist lanced out, smacking against the fellow's jaw while he was still in the air. The man was unconscious before he hit the bottom.

Doc bent, flipped him over, yanked loose a key dangling from a thong on the lizard-hide collar. He fitted the key to the lock of Johnny's leg iron, twisted briefly and Johnny stood free.

Doc grabbed up the whip he had wrested from the guard and, swerving, ducked through the hole into Ham's pit.

"Follow me, Johnny," Doc suggested, cautiously, and reached to unlock Ham's leg iron.

SUDDENLY, from all along the line of fantastic pits, the groans and babblings, the whip-cracking, ceased. One note dominated the nightmare scene: the deep, echoing clangor of a brass gong.

One of the overseers had witnessed his fellow plunge mysteriously into the pit and he had sounded the warning gong. While the dread hush spread over the pit, overseers converged, running, toward the hole where Johnny had been working.

"We'll never make it, Doc," Johnny snapped. "They kill anybody caught trying to escape!"

A cursing uproar burst out, as the first-arriving overseers discovered Johnny's pit to be empty. More of the lizard-collared guards swarmed down. A whip lashed into Ham's pit, as one of the overseers discovered the three men there.

Bellowed words brought the others crowding to the pit rim. Whips lashed down. As Doc lunged upright from unlocking Ham, the pit became a whistling storm of flesh-cutting rawhide.

Doc shoved the leg-iron key to Johnny.

"Follow me through into the next pit and unlock Monk," he shouted above the *swish* and crack of flaying leather.

Close at Doc's heels came Johnny and Ham. While the two bent to the task of releasing Monk, Doc stood upright, taking the rain of whip lashes, cutting back with the whip he had wrested from the first guard.

Under the red volcanic glare, Doc's face, uplifted to the lightning of whips, was a mask of emotionless bronze. He did not use his left arm to fend off the searing strokes. He had better use for that left arm. It coöperated like a machine with his whip-cracking arm.

Doc was not whipping aimlessly. Holding his left arm in such a way that he could protect his eyes, he sent his lash snaking upward from the pit with a twist of his cabled wrist. A deft jerk at the precisely correct instant caused the long, pliant rawhide to curl tightly about whatever object it struck. Sometimes it was a neck. Sometimes an arm or a leg.

But in every instance, a quick, backward jerk of Doc's arm brought his whip-hooked victim toppling into the pit. And then it was that Doc's left fist coöperated, driving against the head of each falling victim, pounding them into senselessness.

And after Doc had dragged some half a dozen men into the pit with relentless precision, the remaining overseers drew back, cursing and shouting, out of range of the appalling rawhide lash.

"O.K., Doc," Johnny's voice sounded.

Monk kicked his loosened leg chain aside. "I'm clear, Doc!"

"Lead the way, Monk," Doc ordered. "Duck through the same hole I first entered by. The rest of you follow. I will hold them off with the whip and bring up the rear."

Monk, crowded closely by Johnny and Ham, butted through

into the next pit back of the active working line. Doc ceased slashing his whip and bent to follow them, only to have his head rammed with a hollow thump against an object hurtling back through the hole from the other direction.

It was Monk's granite head that Doc had bumped.

"We can't get out that way, Doc!" Monk roared, in his frantic haste squirming past Doc and whacking his head on the bottom of the pit as he fell in.

Ham and Johnny came piling through on top of Monk.

"Carnivorous crabs!" Johnny loudly shrieked.

"Man-eating ones!" Ham augmented.

"Big as dogs!" Johnny insisted.

"And millions of 'em!" Monk finished, holding his head.

Chapter XIII

BITS OF HELL

"This way, then!" Doc said, and whipped through the hole into the pit where Ham had been chained.

There was a blur of movement on the pit floor, accompanied by a fearful sound: a metallic clacking.

Then, Monk, coming through the hole in the wake of Doc, found himself jammed into the pit he was trying to leave.

"Blazes!" Monk protested. "What's the matter?"

"This route is barred, too," Doc said.

"Crabs?"

"Right! The pit floor is covered with them."

"They keep 'em in cages somewhere behind the working pits," Ham jerked. "They turn them loose to forestall escapes. I saw one poor blighter go down under a wave of them, last night. They had his bones picked clean in a horribly short time."

The metallic clacking grew louder, coming into the pit with a din like the croaking of thousands of tree frogs.

"That noise is the crabs clackin' their claws," the academic Johnny said, ungrammatically, but forcefully. "They can take a man's finger off with one snip. They climb your legs, all the time hacking you up as if two razors were working on you."

"They're land crabs, too, Doc," Ham put in. "Something like those recorded in parts of Siberia, only bigger. Not as big as dogs, as Johnny said, but bigger than any I ever heard of before. Ferocious as tiger sharks!"

There was a thumping sound on the pit sides.

"Them guys with the dog collars are heavin' rocks!" Monk roared.

Ham's shout blended with Monk's roar. "Here come the crabs!"

"Kick 'em back!" Monk bawled.

"Kick them back yourself!" Ham snapped. "I have no shoes on!"

"Whadda you think I'm wearin'?" Monk growled. "I'm barefooted, too!"

"Block the hole with your head!" Ham suggested, sarcastically.

While they quarreled, they were acting; Monk had picked up one of the large stones which had been heaved into the pit and was smashing crabs as they came in. Ham was slugging at another hole with the weighted butt of the whip which Doc had dropped.

Some of the clack-clacking monsters got through. Johnny was dancing around on his bare feet, trying to stamp on their backs before their fearful claws could nip off his toes or slice through the muscles of his legs.

"Doc," Monk yelled. "They're comin' through faster'n I can pop 'em off!"

"Let a few of them in," the bronze man said, suddenly.

Puzzled, but aware the bronze man must have some plan, Monk complied. Doc, in the meantime, was stripping off his outer garments. He managed to get at the bulletproof chain-mesh undergarment which he wore, and removed it. He used it to shield his hands, grasped one of the crabs when an unusual brightness came into the unholy crimson sky, and straightened. He hurled the fearsome thing at the nearest overseer.

There was light enough for the cruel fellows to see it coming. They emitted cries and crowded into the nearest of honeycomb pits in an effort to escape. The wall of earth between the pits was not wide enough to permit quick, mass action.

Monk got the idea and admitted more crabs, one at a time. Doc grabbed the things, hurled them. The overseers, as a matter of safety, withdrew.

"All right," Doc rapped. "We'll make a break for it, now, let me heave you up."

Monk ran, jumped into the bronze man's clasped hands and Doc gave a jerk, hurtling the apish chemist up to the pit rim.

"Head for the underbrush," Doc called.

Ham and Johnny ran at the bronze man, and Doc heaved them up in the same manner. Then he himself leaped, caught the edge of the pit with one deft arm, drew himself up, and ran across the narrow walls of earth between the honeycomb pits, to join his aids.

THE overseers were already swarming upon them. Strangely enough, the fellows seemed to have no weapons other than the vicious whips. They were handicapped by their very numbers, due to the scarcity of the footing on which they had to work.

"Make it faster," Doc called.

His aids were having trouble. Their feet were bare and the volcanic rock had many of the characteristics of broken glass.

Stones began falling near them, rattling on the brittle rock, occasionally breaking off glassy fragments. Whips lashed, popped.

"Go ahead," Doc directed.

They went on, moving as rapidly as the tangled vegetation would allow. Lower down, the jungle growth became more dense. Matted vines and thorny branches disputed their way. Gigantic orchids, pale flowers of evil in the flickering volcanic light, dangled fleshy petals from overhead. Doc's huge frame often bored a way for the others.

"What's the hurry, Doc?" demanded Monk, puffing.

"Renny and Long Tom and Pat are prisoners at the palace," Doc said, simply.

"Well, why bust our necks in this jungle?" Monk queried. "Let's get on one of the turtle trails."

They were paralleling one of the well-beaten trails. At the moment, the red volcanic light was flaring. Doc moved close to the trail and scanned the way ahead.

"Come," he said, and started on a trot down the ancient path.

"This is better," Monk muttered, lumbering close behind.

Fifty yards ahead, Doc halted abruptly.

"Stand back," he said. "Look!"

He stood well to the side of the trail. His bronzed hand drifted out, plucked at something invisible to the eyes of the others. There was a *swish* of tree branches slicing through air, a glint of metal, a sharp thud.

Doc bent and pulled out of the ground a knife buried to the hilt. His hands moved, unfastening the knife from the branch to which it was deftly attached by means of leather stringing.

"An old Malay trick," he announced. "An animal-hair trigger is strung across the trail, practically invisible even in good light. A sapling is bent back with the knife attached. When the hair is broken by a man walking on the trail, the sapling springs upright, sinking the knife into the stomach of the trail walker."

Monk rubbed apprehensively at his midriff, said nothing.

"These trails are possibly guarded by other traps, also," Doc stated. "By daylight, looking sharply, they might be traversed safely, but at night they had best be left alone."

Doc handed the knife to Ham. "Perhaps you had better carry it till we locate your sword cane."

"That reminds me of something else we lost, Doc," Monk burst in. "Habeas Corpus——"

"That porker getting lost is the only good thing that's happened to anybody on this blasted island," Ham snapped.

"Come," Doc said, forestalling another resumption of the quarrel.

He plunged back into the tangled jungle growth. The others followed. They forged on, working interminably through darkness slashed occasionally by the lurid volcanic light.

It was nearing morning when, through the interstices of jungle vegetation, the grim walls of Count Ramadanoff's palace loomed ahead. On the side toward the sea, the walls were glistening wetly black from high-flung spray. On the jungle side, the towers and turrets of igneous stone were bathed in a bloody mist, as the red volcanic light blanketed through miasmatic swamp vapor.

Monk hunched his massive shoulders. "Spooky-lookin' joint, ain't it?"

"A habitation singularly minacious," Johnny murmured.

Monk, as Johnny's self-appointed interpreter, said: "He means full of threats."

"Everything is threatening on this island," Ham said. "Doc, those pits where we were digging—what's it all about?"

Doc's hand waved out toward the bastioned walls of twenty-feet-thick volcanic rock surrounding the palace.

"The secret of the pits lies behind those walls," he stated.

"You mean that whiskered devil, the count?" Ham queried.

"With the Count Ramadanoff, yes."

Doc stepped a few paces aside, bent over, and straightened up holding a fallen palm trunk thicker than his body.

"Help with this fallen log," he instructed. "If we are to climb that wall, we will have to get it propped over the water in the moat by the wall."

All labored strenuously getting the log solidly against the

wall. Doc tested it with his weight; then standing with legs grimly planted and back braced against the wall, he said, tersely, "Monk! Up on my shoulders."

Monk stepped from Doc's cupped hands to the bronze man's shoulders with a balanced ease surprising for a man so heavily built. With his feet on Doc's shoulders, he braced his back against the wall.

"Next, Ham," Doc said.

Ham mounted swiftly from Doc's hands to the top of his head, from Monk's hands to Monk's shoulders. Standing there, back to the wall, his own upreached hand missed the top of the wall by only a few feet.

"All right, Johnny," Doc called.

"Veritably, an elevating proceeding," Johnny murmured. "Herculean in concept, but destined irrevocably for fructiferous termination."

"Save that until Ham gets off my neck," Monk grumbled.

The professorial Johnny stepped closer and then—monocle, loin cloth and all—skinned up the three-man "rope" with the agility of an acrobat. Gaining the top of the wall, he lay flat to hook his feet over the rear edge, then reached over, grasped Ham's upreaching hands.

Supported by Johnny's grasp Ham swung free from Monk's shoulders. Monk, in turn, grasped Ham's legs. Doc climbed over the dangling human chain and got his hands atop the wall. The wiry Johnny, for a moment, had been sustaining the weight of all of them. Johnny might be an ex-professor and he might wear a monocle, but he was about as toughly muscled an individual as could be found.

When all were on the wall, Doc eased over and hung by his hands from the other side, and, one after the other, his aids climbed over his body, hung from his feet and dropped into the palace courtyard below. Then Doc dropped lightly to join them.

"Lateral peregrinations eminently successful," Johnny whispered.

Doc led the way through inky shadows to a small stone structure which evidently had been intended as quarters for servants. He forced the door and led his aids inside.

"Wait here," he said.

"Where'll you be, Doc?" Monk asked, mystified.

"Going to climb the tower and enter the palace from above. Will open the door from the inside—when you hear my whistle."

Johnny asked, "Does it percolate to this secretive assemblage that the sinister genius of the Galapagos may be simulating nescience of our ensconcement behind his bastioned ramparts?"

"You mean the count might know we're here and he's set a trap for us?" Monk translated.

"Exactly," Johnny agreed.

"Possible," Doc admitted. "This count is diabolically clever."

"And there's that beast—that thing—that monster!" Monk muttered. "There ain't rightly no name for it, Doc."

"It is as large as a house," Ham corroborated.

"Assuredly, yes," Johnny said, "with an infinitesimal exaggeration."

"How close were you to the thing?" Doc questioned.

"Too close!" Monk gulped. "We saw it from the slitted window of the tower."

"Let us hope you hear my whistle," Doc said.

The bronze man took silent steps and was swallowed by crawling shadows. His aids stared tensely in the direction where the palace loomed in the darkness. And when next the red lightning flashed its lurid menace, they saw Doc, flattened like a human fly on the sheer surface of the black tower, climbing by the sheer fabulous strength of fingers and toes the almost non-existent cracks between the stone blocks.

Then the lightning died and blackness swooped down, and when again the red lightning flickered, Doc had disappeared.

Chapter XIV

JUNGLE PALACE

Doc had little difficulty effecting an entrance through one of the high tower windows, for it had no fastening. In the darkness, he felt his way down unbannistered, serpentine steps. In the halfway room containing the long window slit overlooking the courtyard dungeon, he paused and peered out.

Below, in the flagstoned enclosure, the rippling volcanic light revealed to him the same incredible monster that the others had seen. The fearful beast on its shapeless multi-clawed legs was propelling its gross body around, its saw-toothed tail lashing, its armored head wagging. Foam dripped from its grisly jaws as it braced itself against a barred cell, its claws scraping out.

In a frenzy of impotence at its failure to break through the bars, the monster swelled its scabrous body to what appeared to be half again its original size.

Doc Savage, watching, made no sound. His finger drifted out, felt briefly over the glass of the slitted window, then drummed softly.

As though the drumming on the window glass had been a signal, there was a sound in the darkness behind Doc—a breath unwillingly expelled. Doc crouched, jerked out of line of the window and listened.

Through the weighting blackness came sounds of breaths, jerkily taken. Plainly, Doc was sharing this room with some person attempting to conceal the noise of his breathing.

Holding his breath, moving with the utter silence of a jungle denizen, Doc eased toward the source of those bated breathing sounds. His body was crouched, his hand out-stretched, cabled fingers tensed to grip and choke.

Then he stood stock still, sensitive nostrils flaring. A subtle odor, a faint and familiar perfume, wafted to him. The tension went out of his clawed fingers and he straightened, groping in front of him gently.

"Pat," he whispered.

From out of the darkness sounded a smothered gasp and feminine hands grasped for him.

"Oh, Doc," breathed Pat.

Pat Savage was trembling; but with Doc's presence, strength seemed to come back to her. She stopped shaking, sighed and looked up, trying to see the bronze man's face. She shuddered. "Another hour would have been too late. Renny and Long Tom were to be given to the—thing, at daybreak."

"You mean the monster in the court?"

"Yes," Pat said, grimly. "The count locked me in here to watch the—the feeding. He says I'll be the next one." Her voice became more grim. "He's been trying to scare me into agreeing to stay on the island. He says he'll make me a queen. Imagine! Queen of the honeycomb pits. He's not human. He's a fiend! He's more of a monster than that— that thing in the courtyard!"

Then Pat went silent, as the fateful piano music flooded the room, bombarding their ears with weird vibrations, the notes seeming to roll through the darkness with lethal menace.

As suddenly as it had begun, the music stopped; though, as always before, a ominous pulsing hung in the air.

"Some one is going to die!" Pat gasped.

"Why do you say that?" Doc asked, sharply.

"The count plays on his piano—and some one *always* dies!" Pat said, rapidly. "I know it sounds mad. But it is true. Usually, it is the thumb-hole death. A hole appears in your temple, about the size you could press your thumb into!"

Concealed lights flashed on then, bathing the bare rock-girt room with white brilliance. Doc and Pat blinked to accustom their eyes to the sudden glare. Pat gasped at what she saw in the light, shuddered. Doc was equally surprised, but his bronze features remained impassive.

Standing there, so close Doc could reach him with a leap, was the Count Ramadanoff.

In black evening clothes he loomed tall and sinister, his Czar-of-Russia beard an inky-black against his long white face. Broader than his brother Boris, nearly two feet taller, he was in other respects identical in appearance, even to the rings on his tapering fingers, a ruby and an emerald, each as big as the end of a man's thumb.

Doc watched the count's eyes—as hard and glittering as the gems on his fingers. Doc had power that but few men had succeeded in developing down through the ages. He could use his gold-flake eyes upon another, often to hypnotize against the other's will.

But with the count, Doc got nowhere. The brittle, gem-like eyes glared back as though they did not see at all. The count's lips twitched slightly. He made a low and courtly bow. His white hand waved out, the jewels flashing.

He spoke suavely: "If you will be so gracious as to escort the lady, early morning breakfast is served in the great hall."

Pat said, with her lips only, "He does the queerest things. This is some kind of trap."

Doc nodded without speaking, rested his fingers against Pat's elbow and guided her through the opened door and down the winding stone steps. The count followed closely, as they pushed through the hanging drapes of ruby velvet on the stair landing and entered the cavernous maw which was the hall.

Before the huge fireplace where the blue flames danced without sound, without heat, without appreciable light, a breakfast table was set for three.

"You see, I have prepared for you," the count said, nodding them to chairs.

THE breakfast table with its crisp damask and softly glowing silver service was the only fresh touch in the high-raftered hall. All else remained the same: the grand piano swathed in sea otter, the swinging candelabra burning in hundreds of flames, the regal collection of samovars, sending off dull metal glitters from velvet-draped recesses.

While slaves served the food, the count leaned forward and said in a confiding manner:

"You are a man of the world enough to know that things are not always as they appear."

"And so?" Doc said, noncommittally.

"It would appear that I have treated your aids badly," the other murmured. "Such is not the case.

"Three of your men I consigned to my pits," the count continued. "Strange as it may seem, I did it to protect them from an island horror."

"The thumb-hole death?" Doc suggested.

The bearded giant murmured, "Ah, you know of it?"

"I had occasion to observe its deadly effect in New York."

The count's eyes glittered. "It has long hovered over brother Boris."

"And what have you to say regarding my other two men?" Doc questioned, dryly.

Their host drawled, "My dear fellow, they are at this minute leading a searching party to recover your body, supposedly mangled by sharks."

Pat interposed hotly, "If that is true, why was I locked in the tower room and told to watch their executions?"

"A proceeding later to be illumined," the count said precisely. "The intended executions—a myth."

"There was no myth about that—that monster I saw in the courtyard!" Pat insisted. She was not eating.

The count helped himself to food. He leaned toward Doc. "You have seen my pet?"

"The creature in the courtyard?" Doc questioned. "The iguana?"

The count's breath drew in raspingly. "So—you were able to identify it!" He shrugged. "Identifying it, you must have been all the more impressed by its formidable size. A Galapagos, or seagoing, lizard, attaining the length of six feet, would normally be considered a monster. You saw my pet in the courtyard. How long would you estimate him to be?"

"It appeared," Doc admitted, "many times that size."

"But how is it possible?" Pat protested.

She was not eating. She had no taste for food served in the sinister environment of the palace. The blue flames in the fireplace, instead of lighting up her lovely face, threw it in ghastly, bluish shadow.

Pat shrank back as the count's tapering fingers reached out to touch her arm.

"On this island are undreamed horrors," he murmured.

"And something else," Doc put in. "Something you wish found."

For the first time, something other than sinister evil seemed to come over the man before them. He straightened visibly in his chair and put down his eating implements.

"You have learned of that?" he asked.

"It has become evident," Doc Savage told him.

The big man leaned forward, smiling eagerly in his black beard. "You know what it is?"

"The name?—yes," the bronze man admitted. "The Devil's Honeycomb."

"You don't know more than that?" the other demanded.

"No," Doc admitted.

The bearded man settled back and seemed relieved. He began eating again, glancing once at them curiously, as if noting for the first time that they were consuming no food. He did not urge them to eat.

"I have need of your scientific abilities," said the count, casually. "I have tried the usual instruments for making subterranean surveys. They are not sufficiently sensitive. You can make more powerful ones, more delicate ones."

Doc Savage said, sharply, "In order to properly design the instruments, it will be necessary to know what you want located."

"That is impossible," the other said, abruptly.

"Then what you ask me to do is also impossible," Doc informed him.

The bearded man showed his teeth through his heavy whiskers.

"You have the reputation of a man who does the impossible," the count said, grimly. "You will manage to do it now, or take some very unpleasant consequences."

Doc Savage said nothing.

"With your exhaustive knowledge of geology and cartography, my dear Savage, it should not be too difficult for you to locate an object which I shall describe as having an atomic structure entirely different from the rest of the island," the whiskered man said.

The count raised his napkin and blotted his thin lips. He blotted carefully. For a moment, the whole lower half of his face was concealed by the stiff damask.

The blue flames which leaped in the fireplace commenced promptly to shorten. They died down to half their height, within the next few seconds.

Doc Savage spoke suddenly to Pat in strange language— words composed largely of guttural, though curiously melodic, sounds. Doc was using the language of the ancient Mayans, the remarkable people whose civilization flourished in the Yucatan peninsula of Mexico long before the Egyptian pyramids were built.

It is doubtful if more than a dozen persons in the so-called civilized world were sufficiently conversant with the strangely syllabled speech to understand it.

EVEN as Doc talked, the blue flames shortened farther until they became little more than crawling stubs within the massive fireplace.

"What are you saying?" the count demanded. His voice had a noticeable nasal quality now.

"Nothing," Pat answered, tensely. She sat back in her chair, breathing deeply as Doc, speaking in Mayan, had directed her to do.

"Fill your lungs with fresh air," Doc had said. "And if the blue flame goes out, do not take another breath until we can get outside."

To the Count Ramadanoff, Doc said in English: "Before I do anything about locating your Devil's Honeycomb, the release of my two men held prisoners in your iguana pit will be necessary."

"So?" the count said, with nasal quality still predominantly in his voice. "You have finished with breakfast chatter? You prefer to deal in realities? Then listen to this: Not only do I refuse to release your two men, but I am pleased to inform you that your other three aids are prisoners of mine also—securely locked in that same garden shelter where you left them when you scaled my tower.

"This palace, my dear Savage, is amply equipped with electrical safeguards, much in the manner, I should judge, as your own skyscraper headquarters in New York is protected. Nothing can happen within these walls that I am not immediately informed about."

Turning his head, the count summoned a slave by means of that odious hissing noise he made through compressed lips.

"Throw open the outside door," he ordered.

The slave, swarthy, of mixed blood, padded across the hall, swung wide the massive door and started back toward the breakfast table. Thirty feet from the door, his body was gripped with spasmodic convulsions. A chopped-off scream of agony passed his lips as his face contorted and his body, grotesquely knotted, thumped onto the floor. Early morning sunlight slanted through the open door, bathing his heaped body with funereal benediction.

The count's eyes glittered. "If you doubt he is dead, my dear Savage, you have my special permission to examine the body. And anyone else who approaches within that thirty-foot area in front of the door, will be similarly electrocuted. I arranged the exhibition to demonstrate to you the futility of attempting escape."

From the region of the fireplace sounded a metallic sigh, as the blue flames flickered out. Out of the tail of her eye, Pat had been watching the flames. She held her breath. Doc did the same.

As Doc was aware, the failing of the blue flames signaled

the flooding of the room with an anæsthetizing, perhaps even a lethal, gas.

As a flame in a gas stove burns blue, giving off virtually no illumination, so did the weird flames in the count's fireplace burn blue and lightlessly. That they gave off no heat was accounted for by drafts mechanically arranged to conduct the heat up the chimney.

But the draft, controlled by a concealed floor button within reach of the count's toe at the breakfast table, could be closed and the flames extinguished, throwing such a volume of unburned gas into the great hall that, even with the outside door opened, a few whiffs would rob a person of consciousness.

Doc had been warned when his alert eyes had observed the count pressing the napkin to his lips. Under cover of the napkin, the count had inserted, no doubt, wads of chemically treated gauze into his nostrils so that he could breath for a short time with safety in the gas-laden atmosphere. It was this gauze that had given his voice its pronounced nasal quality.

Coincident with the failing of the blue flames, a loud crash sounded. It was the breakfast table going over, propelled by a forcible kick from Doc's feet. The table turned over in the direction of the count and with such appalling force that the count, in his chair, went over also.

In the moment that the bearded man was clearing himself of the table wreckage, Doc grabbed Pat by the arm and propelled her violently across the room and up the sweeping flight of stone steps.

The count was on his feet and running forward by the time Doc and Pat had reached the stair landing, hung with the velvet drapes. The count looked very happy as he observed that the ruby-colored drapes had tangled themselves about the fugitives and must certainly trip them up.

But Doc and Pat were not tripped by the hangings. It was no accident that the drapes had become swathed about Doc's mounting figure. Doc was holding them in one metallic hand, carrying them upward with him.

Suddenly he stopped, faced around. "Hang onto my back," he said in Mayan to Pat. "And hold your breath."

Pat thrust arms about Doc's neck from behind. From high overhead, the brass hoops creaked on their rod and the ruby drapes became taut as a wind-bellied sail, as Doc, lifting his feet and gripping the drape like a rope, swung downward in a wide arc.

Down he swung on that plunging curve, passing high over the astonished face of the count and up, up, with Pat clinging tightly around his neck. At the very height of his swing, he was dangling at a fearful distance above the high-swung candelabra.

He let go his hold on the drape and hurtled forward and down, the wind a hard rush in his ears. His muscle-corded hand, outstretched, caught the candelabra, his momentum swinging it forward. Candles showered down, their flames whipping like tiny comets' tails.

Letting go of the candelabra, the man of bronze swooped through the air above that death stretch—the thirty feet of flooring in front of the door charged with high-amperage electricity. Through the lofty door his body shot, down. He landed easily, taking the shock in a way that showed he had practiced jumping from great heights.

Pat had managed to hang on throughout.

Chapter XV

MANGROVE MURDER

SAFELY outside that palace of death, Doc circled the tower, running; and Pat ran with him. It was Doc's intention to reach the tomblike structure in the garden where his aids were imprisoned, and effect their release.

But Doc did not reach the prison house. He got close enough that Monk, Ham and Johnny, all three, could see him from the barred window. Ham even shrieked a warning. But it was too late.

A black fury, which had leaped down from a palace window, landed with crushing weight on Doc's shoulders. Doc went down, a hard fall to the flagstoned yard, and on top of him, riding him down, was the figure of Count Ramadanoff.

The count's fists thudded on Doc with vicious short-arm jabs, delivered with the force of a pile-driver. His white hands that looked so soft, were not soft at all. On his short cut through the palace to intercept Doc, he had slipped his hands into gloves of basket-weave wire, as flexible as thin kid and knobbed on the knuckles with jagged slugs of lead.

"With my own hands, I will beat you to death!" the count raged. "Three of your men at one time my fists have beaten —and now you!"

As Doc's head hit the flagstoned surface, the count's right fist bludgeoned in. There was nothing short-arm about this jab. He had timed the blow. His fist bashed in from far back, with all the weight of his massive shoulders behind it. He meant to crush Doc's skull between mailed fist and flagstone.

The fist drove down, struck solidly—but not on Doc's head. Doc jerked clear, timing his movement so that the count could not pull his punch. The fist swished air in Doc's face and rammed flagstone. Holes had been fashioned in the backs of the leaded gloves so the finger rings could push through and serve as additional punishment factors.

Under the drive of fist against flagstone, the ruby, as big as the end of a man's thumb, crushed into a mound of reddish crystalline powder.

Doc, as he jerked clear, drove his own fist upward to the point of the count's chin. The madman's head rocked back till his bull neck creaked; and Doc doubled his knee and kicked himself clear.

Up on their feet, the two crashed in at each other. Doc took one fearful blow on the side of his head, but he rolled with it, thereby avoiding most of its effect and, at the same time, providing an opening for his own fists. He hit three times in dazzling succession. It was almost like a single blow; a drilling one-two punch over the heart and an uppercut to the jaw swung from down around his knees. The blow would have dropped a rhinoceros.

It dropped Count Ramadanoff senseless.

He did not awaken until several minutes later; and by that time, his hands were tied. Doc, guided by Pat, had found the generator room and turned off the electricity all over the palace. Also, by the use of a tiny vest-pocket grenade, he had broken down the door of the garden prison and freed his three aids.

THE count sat up groggily, and Doc ordered, "Inside the palace! Free my two men locked in your dungeon cells."

"And make it fast," Monk threatened.

With the count leading and the others following close, they trooped through the great hall and up the winding stairs.

"You have beaten me with your fists," the count said. "Very well; but there is still the thumb-hole death."

Before the door to the balcony which surrounded the animal pit, the count paused, impressively.

"What you will see beyond this door is something the like of which, until today, has never been observed by any living man except myself," he announced, dramatically.

"I know what we'll see," Monk blazed. "The monster!"

"Not the monster you have in mind," Doc interposed, enigmatically.

The count's breath rasped. "So you have solved my mystery?"

"Correct," Doc admitted. "The window which looks upon this courtyard from the tower room is, in reality, a powerful magnifying glass. The beast we saw is not as large as it appears."

The count's lips writhed. "Do not make the mistake of thinking the horror is diminished. It is increased uncounted times."

Pat shuddered. "What could be worse than that—monster?"

The count leered at her. His answer was simple—and devastating.

"Many monsters," he said.

His foot must have touched a hidden lever, actuated mechanically, for the door to the balcony swung open. Doc's aids crowded forward and stopped with ludicrous suddenness, staring down into the pit with cold shock.

Monk was the first one to get his voice.

"Not one monster!" he gasped. "But about a hundred of 'em, all nearly six feet long!"

The hundred was somewhat of an exaggeration, because the iguanas, the most hideous of beasts, were so tightly packed on the dungeon floor that their scaly hides rubbed together and made it impossible for them to swell out their bodies in the loathsome habit they had in moments of excitement.

The mass of scabrous-hided monsters undulated on the flagstoned floor, snorting, armored heads without exception pointing toward the cell wherein Renny and Long Tom were held captive.

"They have been starved to hunger frenzy," the count's odious voice sounded. "They are waiting for the bars to go up, so that they may get inside the cell."

Pat uttered a choked cry of dismay.

The count's silky voice, thick with expected triumph, continued: "Iguanas inhabiting some of the Galapagos Islands are not particularly savage, I believe. These are different. Everything on this island is savage. If I did not find it so when I came, I made it so.

"You will observe, for one thing, these brutes are a full foot longer than the average. The strongest—those fellows which have forged their way to the front and are grinding their teeth against the bars—are half again larger than any other iguana reported on other islands."

"Tryin' to throw a scare into us, huh?" Monk blustered, secure in the realization that the electricity had been cut off and that the count could no longer control the bars by a touch of a hidden button.

"If anything happens to my men——" Doc began, ominously.

"Your warning comes too late, my dear Savage," the count rasped. "Look!"

BEFORE their horrified eyes, the iron bars commenced to lift upward out of the floor. There was a gobbling sound— the count's weird laugh.

"Fools!" he raved. "What matters it if you have temporarily disrupted my electrical system? There are a hundred places on this balcony where I can touch my toe and actuate the bars by mechanical control!"

As the bars lifted upward, the slavery-jawed iguanas surged like a wave inside the cell.

Renny and Long Tom, acting in a way they had planned for just that emergency, leaped upward, caught hold of the rising bars. The bars ceased lifting and the two men hung, sag-weighted, while the scabrous monsters, with frenzied grunts and a blood-chilling grate of serrated teeth, leaped up at them, falling just short.

The count continued his gobbling laugh.

"It is always the same!" he gloated. "The victims hang onto the bars until the weight of their bodies loosens their grip. The monsters then have their fun. Observe how the iguanas crowd from behind. The two men will not be enough to appease them. So you, my dear Savage, with your three other aids and your charming cousin, will form a second course for my pets, I confidently predict."

Doc's gold-flecked eyes were lancing around the torture chamber. He could not reach his aids by means of the circular balcony. A sheer dividing wall cut off the way. And by the time he could circle the palace, forcing doors, it would be too late. Long Tom and Renny, their bodies grown leaden, would have lost their grips and fallen prey to rending jaws and claws.

There was but one way to the cell. That way led directly through the pit where the monsters crowded together.

Doc looked at Johnny. "Hold your knife at the count's neck! If he makes a move—— Monk, you and Ham stand by."

Swerving, Doc gripped the balcony railing and vaulted down into the pit, along with the swarming, hunger-crazed monsters.

"Doc!" Ham shouted in horror.

Ham's voice was lost in the beastly chorus of grunts echoing up as the iguanas discovered the human in their midst.

Pat suddenly hid her eyes. Had she watched, she would have seen some interesting footwork. Doc landed on the scaled backs of one of the creatures. As it lurched, he leaped onto the back of another. Four opened mouths rushed him. He leaped clear, in rapid succession stepping from back to back of the close-pressed animals, much in the manner of a white-water timber-jack running over a log jam.

By virtue of expert eye-to-muscle coördination, never remaining more than a split-second in any one spot, Doc reached the middle of that nightmarish arena. From then on, progress was easier. The animals were too closely packed to attack him successfully, so long as he kept on his feet and moving.

Doc reached the cell. Leaping from the back of the enraged iguanas to grip the iron bars, he pulled himself up to a safe height. Then, bracing his feet against one bar, hands gripping another, he exerted all his tremendous strength in an effort to pry them apart.

Under the appalling force of his muscular pressure, the loose ends of the bars shuddered, then bent.

"Can you squeeze through now?" he demanded.

Long Tom did not have to answer. His bean-pole body had already writhed through. Holding to the bars, he added his own strength to that of Doc's. The bars bent enough more to permit Renny also to squirm through. Hand over hand, the three climbed the bars and pulled themselves over the railing to the balcony floor.

Looking back across that frightful pit of frustrated monsters, Doc called to his aids, "Wait till we come to you!"

Doc used a vest-pocket bomb—tiny things, they were; no bigger than medicinal capsules, but loaded with a powerful explosive—and blew down a door which separated the balcony from the rest of the palace. Where necessary, he used more of the capsule bombs to force other doors, and reached his aids.

United now for the first time since the Devil's Honeycomb mystery had flung malignant shadows across them, Doc, his five aids, and Pat, with Ramadanoff their prisoner, went on a quick, triumphant tour of the palace.

They found the palace empty, the slaves having decamped into the jungle at the first opportunity.

"WE'RE all together at last," Pat said, joyfully.

"Yeah, all but Habeas Corpus," Monk amended, a dour look on his homely face.

"I favor leaving the island quickly," Ham snapped. "Before that hog finds us!"

"You shyster!" Monk growled. "Habeas Corpus is a *good* hog."

"Good to eat, maybe. But I doubt even that."

After providing themselves with firearms, Doc's aids donned some of the count's clothes. The count wore nothing apparently, but black. Long Tom pointed at Renny's long, puritanical face protruding from a black waistcoat.

Doubling with laughter, Long Tom said, "You look like *Frankenstein!*"

"Anyhow, they fit," Renny growled. "And I don't look like a scarecrow in a garden patch, like you."

Monk and Ham made acrid comments on each other's appearance.

"Holy cow!" Renny rumbled. "It's sure swell to hear you two guys scrappin' again. This lug that calls himself a count, fixed up some skeletons with some of your clothes hangin' bloody on 'em, and we thought you had all been killed."

As they were all in the act of leaving the palace, Ham pounced upon the blade of his sword cane, where it had been concealed beneath the sea-otter robes on the piano. He examined the tip, found it still coated with the sleep-producing chemical, and shifted the blade back into the malacca cane handle.

Monk sighed. "Now absolutely everything is found but Habeas."

"And he won't be found." Ham said, hopefully. "Didn't you hear the count say the island is infected by fierce things?"

Monk insisted, "Habeas'll never be devoured by anything, on account of he'll do the devourin' himself, if any."

VOLCANIC smoke hung over the island in a black pall, dimming the equatorial sun as Pat, Doc, his aids, and their prisoner hurried from the palace courtyard.

"Now what?" Long Tom muttered.

Doc Savage studied the volcano for a time. Its glow seemed to have acquired additional brilliance.

"That volcano is not behaving in a manner calculated to inspire peace of mind," Doc said. "However, there are two things requiring our immediate attention."

"One is to rescue those poor devils digging those honeycomb pits," Ham offered.

"Right," Doc admitted.

"And the other," Johnny said tensely, for once using small

words, "is to find out what this Devil's Honeycomb business is all about."

"Right again," Doc agreed.

As the party plunged into a grove of mangroves, Doc and the scholarly Johnny conversed in lowered tones.

"No doubt, you have already reached the conclusions that I am going to outline," Johnny said. "First, Ramadanoff insisted you could locate this Devil's Honeycomb, whatever it is, with instruments. That means the Devil's Honeycomb is composed of substance different from the island and volcanic ash."

"Exactly," Doc Savage agreed. "And the fact that those pits are being dug close together indicates that the Devil's Honeycomb, whatever it is, is not large. If it was a large object, they would have dug the pits farther apart."

"I had not thought of that, but it bears out my theory," Johnny declared. "Now have you noticed the geologic structure of this island? That coastal plateau is really a ridge along the shore. That is where they are digging. I am positive the plateau was thrown up as a deposit of volcanic ash. This occurred not many years ago, judging from the lack of vegetation. Beyond the plateau, inland, is a small swamp section, heavily jungled."

Doc Savage put in, "There are indications that the swamp was originally the seashore."

Johnny chuckled. "I see you have reached the same conclusions as myself. Are we going to look the place over?"

"We are," Doc Savage told him. "We are going to examine that swamp quite thoroughly."

Monk dropped back to grumble, "I wish somebody'd tell me what all of those honeycomb pits are for."

"Did the overseers examine the volcanic ash you excavated from the pits?" Doc Savage queried.

"Sure," Monk said. "But not very closely."

"The purpose of those pits may prove to be somewhat of a surprise," Doc Savage said, and offered no more.

As the party proceeded, the mangroves grew more dense. The coiled roots were head-high in places, causing frequent stumbles in the spongy, water-logged soil. The volcanic smoke grew blacker. The red flashes became more lurid. A fine ash of volcanic pumice sifted down through the maze of weirdly curved tree branches above.

Uttering raucous alarms, frigate birds and fantail gulls skimmed over the tops of the giant mangroves. Red-footed boobies perched on their nests and squawked continually.

"These birds would drive a guy nuts!" Monk rumbled.

"They're sure to give us away, in case anybody's looking for us," Long Tom added.

"Snipers in these mangroves is one thing we don't have to worry about," Monk mumbled. "The count was afraid to let any one else on the island have a gun——"

"Down!" Doc rapped, unexpectedly. "Everybody! Get down!"

Monk, with the others, instantly dropped on all fours. A moment later, there was a crash of rifles. Lead snarled through the mangroves, chipping bark, tearing at boughs over their heads.

"My mistake about the snipers," Monk said, grimly.

Chapter XVI

PORTUGUESE FREEBOOTER

Doc and his men returned the fire with the guns they had confiscated from the palace. With the sifting volcanic ash turning the shadowed mangroves into a place of perpetual night, the enemy guns flared in saffron bursts. Echoes crashed flatly.

"Holy cow!" Renny boomed. "Sounds like an army!"

Doc Savage said, "My guess is that brother Boris has flown here from Cocos Island and rounded up the slaves."

Renny groaned. "We should have let Boris drop when he was on the end of that rope hanging from the airplane!"

Monk fired a burst of three shots. Answering bullets chopped mangrove branches about his head.

"Trouble with firing at their gun flashes is, they shoot back at yours," Monk growled.

The battle went on, the mangroves rocking to gun thunder, and the black volcanic dust sifting down as though trying to blot out the livid bloom of guns. Lead whined and smacked, driving the combatants to seek additional protection by burrowing deeper in the mud.

"Monk's pig would love this!" the fastidious Ham gritted, bogged almost to his eyebrows.

Big-fisted Renny growled, "Let's charge 'em!"

Suddenly the enemy firing increased, coming noticeably closer.

"They're charging *us!*" Renny boomed.

"Keep down!" Doc ordered. Doc spoke calmly, hiding the alarm he must have felt. As a matter of fact, they were on as deadly a spot as any they had run against on the island. With lead slapping around them like hail, there was a good chance of none of them escaping.

"Let's charge 'em!" Renny roared again.

Johnny's scholastic voice said sharply. "Exsiccate, and attune auditory faculties."

"Huh?" Renny gulped, startled. "Whatcha say?"

"He means for you to dry up and listen," Monk interpreted.

Listening, they heard clearly above the whooping gun thunder a new sound, a massed grunting, as though perhaps a hundred or more of the count's hunger-crazed iguanas had escaped from the palace and were butting through the mangroves on a man-hunt.

The Count Ramadanoff, himself, was first to name correctly the sound. He did so with considerable excitement.

"Climb trees!" he bawled, abruptly concerned over his own safety. "I will call at our enemies to cease shooting!"

"What's comin'?" Monk demanded.

"The little wild hogs!" the count gasped. "They run in droves like peccaries; in sufficient numbers, they can bring down anything that lives!"

THEY listened. It was a herd of the ferocious little animals, undoubtedly. There was a good deal of noise in the mud.

The count was screaming at the enemy riflemen, beseeching them not to shoot, to climb trees themselves and seek safety. The response was interesting, for it seemed that Doc Savage's party had taken shelter in the only large trees immediately convenient, and that those where the besiegers lay, although thick enough for excellent concealment, were only bushes which would hardly support human weight.

In a mud-slogging wave, the herd of wild pigs approached.

"The trees!" Doc Savage directed, and they hauled themselves out of the mud and climbed, boosting the big, bearded count up into the branches, helping Pat, the rest of them following hastily.

Ham, always concerned with his appearance, paused to scrape some of the mud off, with the result that he was slow in reaching a tree. In fact, before he gained his tree, a lean, ungainly shote with long legs and flapping sail-like ears popped out of the brush and headed straight for Ham. The mud-smeared lawyer unlimbered his sword cane as he retreated hastily.

"Hey!" Monk bawled. "Be careful! That's Habeas!"

"What of it?" Ham snapped. "If I don't get him, that pack of wild hogs chasing him will!"

"Chasing him, nothing!" Monk bellowed. "Habeas, he's leadin' that gang of hogs!"

Monk's prediction proved to be optimistic. He had based it, no doubt, on Habeas's previous accomplishments in fighting; which had been considerable. But Habeas, in these wild, peccary-like island hogs, had encountered—if not singly, at least in numbers—his match. He could outrun them, however, and he was engaged in doing it.

Ham went up his tree and Habeas promptly tried to climb after him, but failed.

"Scat!" Ham yelled. "Go away! Take your friends with you!"

An idea seized Monk. He hung down, at risk of falling out of his own leafy retreat, and waved an arm, whooping to get Habeas's attention. Monk had long ago taught his pet shote to move in response to hand gestures.

"Take 'em away, Habeas!" Monk yelled, indicating the shote should go in the direction of the enemy attacking party.

Habeas Corpus acquitted himself royally. Promptly setting off at a wild pace, he took his troubles in the shape of a grunting, snorting, tusk-flashing horde of wild pigs, in his wake.

Among the enemy there was much excited shouting, shooting, and an enraged squealing from the pigs. Doc Savage waited until the peccary stragglers joined what sounded like a considerable warfare ahead.

"Come on!" the bronze man said, sharply. "Now is our chance to get clear!"

They scrambled down out of the boughs. Making their escape did not prove to be difficult, because the men who had been besieging them were involved, for the time being, with the herd of wild hogs.

Doc Savage's party pressed for considerable time through the tangled growth and finally came out in what amounted to a valley. Before the last volcanic eruption—if Johnny's geologic observations were as accurate as they should be—the valley had been the shores of a bay.

Doc Savage listened for some time. He heard no sounds of enemies.

"Wait here," he directed the party.

The next moment he was gone into the lurid gloom. He traveled swiftly, setting a course for a definite spot—the beach near where his plane had crashed. Once there, he stripped off his outer garments and entered the surf.

The tide, fortunately, had changed, and the rips were not bad as he swam out to the spot where his plane had sunk. It was impossible more than to approximate the location, which meant that Doc had to make a number of dives before he located the craft in some four fathoms of water. In truth, a film of oil on the surface, coming up from the crashed plane, led the bronze man to the location of the ship.

He dived to it a number of times, and when he swam back to shore, he was heavily burdened.

"Holy cow!" Renny exploded, when Doc joined them in the valley that had formerly been a bay. "Whatcha got?"

"Our devices for locating metals underground," Doc Savage told him. "Long Tom—Johnny—you can help with this."

The apparatus was sensitive, but was unimpaired by submersion; its case had been waterproof. They worked with it for three hours. Then Doc Savage went and stood on a particular spot.

"Here," he said.

It was near the beginning rise of the coastal ridge and was in volcanic ash. They dug in, using sticks for implements, working as quietly as possible. It was Monk whose stick first hit buried wood. He scraped madly and uncovered a porthole.

"Pirate treasure!" he gulped, excitedly.

Doc Savage held a match close to the porthole to examine it, then said, "Look," and pointed at an inscription on the porthole rim.

The inscription read:

Patented June 1, 1908

"Pirates," Doc Savage said, "were put out of business before 1908."

The porthole was large; and after they had broken out the glass and worked the rim free, they could by squeezing get inside. Doc posted Renny and Monk as guards. Doc, with the others, managed to get inside.

They searched carefully and at length, and found nothing to indicate this was anything but an old tramp steamer. The boat had a metal hull; most of the bulkheads were of steel; and there were no skeletons about. The hull was mutilated enough to show the ship had been wrecked—probably driven high on the shore in the course of a storm, or by a tidal wave.

"This has turned out to be a bust," Long Tom complained.

Only the count registered no disappointment. Doc, observing the bearded man covertly, noted that, strangely enough, the fellow could not keep from his face a look of feverish triumph.

Shortly after this, the count approached Doc, complaining that the ropes hurt his wrists and he might as well be freed, since the only exit from the wreck—the porthole—was guarded by Renny and Monk.

Doc removed the bonds, at the same time remarking, "If you try to escape, the results may not be pleasant."

The count bowed, narrowing his eyes to hide a gleam of triumph. He moved to one side, and Johnny and Pat promptly assailed Doc with misgivings.

"Why did you do it?" Pat demanded. "He was lying about his wrists hurting him."

Doc's expression was enigmatic. "Pretend not to notice him."

Doc SAVAGE himself pretended to be occupied in another part of the wreck. The count, when he judged himself to be unobserved, slunk from sight, entering a portion of the wrecked hull formerly used as the captain's cabin.

The count found the spot for which his fingers were feeling. His tapering fingers pressed. A small panel slid open. He thrust his hand through the hole, felt behind the bulkhead, and drew his hand out quickly, holding something.

"Give it to me!" Doc ordered, and advanced on the bearded man.

The count snarled, his bearded face contorted in baffled rage. Then, quickly, he controlled himself, forced a grim smile.

"Take it," he growled. "But I warn you, it means death!"

He placed the article in Doc's outstretched hand.

"Outside," Doc ordered, and the count walked out.

"Tie him up again," Doc directed Johnny.

Only after the count's arms were again bound did the bronze man allow his attention to be distracted to the object in his hand. It was a mariner's emergency hand compass, studded on the back with two superb stones, much like those which had graced the count's finger rings. An emerald and a ruby!

Unexpectedly, wafting on the pumice-fogged air, the bronze man's trilling note came, causing Pat and Johnny to flash startled looks. Doc held the compass out for Pat to see.

"What is it?" Pat asked. She frowned, "I don't get it."

"The engraving," Doc suggested.

"It's in Russian," Pat decided. "I'm not so good at Russian."

"It says merely that the compass was presented to the

Count Ramadanoff by the Czar of Imperial Russia," Doc told her. "It is the date which is important."

"I'll be superamalgamated!" Johnny exploded. "The date is 1911!"

Chapter XVII

THE RED RING

"RIGHT," Doc said. "The date is 1911."

His words were echoed by a rumbling sound, like caged thunder. No wind blew. The noise seemed to press down with the sifting black pumice, and at the same time to ooze up through the ground. It was everywhere—as though tortured rocks, far below the earth's surface, were vibrating throughout the globe.

"What is it?" Pat gasped.

"The volcano," Doc said.

"The exordium of the termination," Johnny remarked.

"I get that one," Pat said tensely. "The beginning of the end."

"We must drop everything," Doc said, "and hurry ahead to rescue those poor devils in the pits."

Doc led off, his aids and Pat trailing after him, bringing big, bearded Ramadanoff. Out of the jungle tangle, forging ahead through jagged lava beds, Doc's party was within close view of the squat volcanic cone. The mountain's mouth was wreathed in lurid light and smoke belched upward in a twisting spiral, to mushroom against high clouds and sift its pumice over the entire island.

"It won't be long now!" Ham yelled.

"She's been buildin' for a bust ever since we've been here!" Monk agreed, loudly.

Doc slowed his giant strides to fall back alongside Pat. When no one was observing, he placed the jeweled compass in her hands.

"Keep it where it will be safe," he admonished.

"You must be expecting violent action!" Pat gasped.

Doc said nothing, possibly because ahead, from out of

gloom created by the black ash, gun flashes stabbed redly, like tiny, erupting volcanoes.

"Down!" Doc shouted. Bullets slammed whining past.

"BROTHER Boris again!" Monk squawked.

The volcanic rock afforded innumerable crevices. Concealing themselves, Doc and his aids returned enough fire to keep the enemies at a distance. Of even greater danger than the smashing lead, was the brittle volcanic slag which broke into thousands of pieces under impact of bullets, showering the slivered rock around like glassy needles.

Doc issued strict orders against reckless exposure on the part of any of his aids; then, leaving Monk and Ham and Pat in charge of the prisoner, he took the others with him to stage a flanking movement.

Taking advantage of lava gullies and dead, gas craters, Doc's flanking party worked up close. Once they were sighted, and a burst of bullets hunted them. One slug felled a high torch thistle and slapped the frightful plant across Renny's shoulders, which meant Renny would spend weeks picking the barbs from his skin. Bullets splattered volcanic glass, drove splinters.

Doc left them, merging away into the gloom. The volcanic ash was falling thicker now and the squat volcano cone was bathed in a perpetual rose glow. Appearing to ooze from the rock under foot, that fearful rumble, like caged thunder, came again.

Then came a crashing roar. Different sound! It sent echoes ricocheting through the lava canyons like a dynamite blast.

"Doc's little capsule grenades!" Renny boomed.

Piercing the ash-laden air on the heels of the explosion echoes, stabbed frantic shouts. A ragged burst of gunfire came from Boris Ramadanoff's men. These noises receded until there was only silence and the sifting black snow, and the mountain top gleaming a fiery red.

Rock crunched, and Doc loomed toward them from out of the murk.

"Foray was eminently successful?" Johnny suggested.

Doc nodded. "They're on the run."

"We better be, too," Renny grumbled. "The whole top of that mountain's about due to blow off, if you ask me."

"It is becoming more threatening every minute," Doc admitted, gravely. "Come on; we'll join the others."

But Doc's flanking party did not join the others. The others joined them! That is, part of the others did.

"Doc!" Monk and Ham roared together, as they came plunging out of the gloom.

"Here!" Doc called, sharply.

"The count's gone!" Ham squalled.

"With Pat!" Monk bellowed.

"He cut his hands free on this glassy rock, I guess," Ham gasped. "And he grabbed Pat!"

Monk howled in rage, "We couldn't shoot on account he held her in front of him."

"And in this dust and murk, he was out of sight in about six steps," Ham finished. "We tried to find him, but no luck."

"Go on to the pits," Doc directed. "Let me hunt Pat."

With a parting wave of his hand, the bronze man moved quickly away. He was out of sight in a few long strides.

WHILE Doc's aids raced for the honeycomb pits, the underground thunder sounded again and the rosy light glowing above the volcano crater expanded violently, flinging fiery streaks through the ashy gloom and disgorging a torrent of lava, which cascaded in red streams down the blunt mountainside.

"I said she was ready to blow," Renny grunted.

Johnny, the geologist, reassured them. "It would be excessively rare for the initial eruption to be of sufficient volume to inundate the plateau where the honeycomb pits are."

Long Tom gasped, "Look!"

"Blazes!" Monk blurted. "Run!"

The warning was hardly necessary. Oozing down a defile upon them came a mass of red, liquid lava. It was a moving serpent of liquid, superheated rock which, disgorged from the gutted earth, had cascaded down the outside of the squat volcanic cone and was now seething forward. Heat in gaseous billows fanned out ahead of the molten avalanche. Doc's aids felt the withering blast, as they climbed in a frenzy toward higher ground.

"Holy cow!" Renny gulped. "That was close!"

"And how are we gonna get back across that strip of melted hells?" Monk wanted to know.

"We're only cut off on one side," Long Tom pointed out.

Nearing the pits, Doc's aids fired warning shots. The overseers, having no firearms, did not contest their advance. Already filled with dread at sight of the volcanic activity, the overseers, shouting in panic, surrendered. Doc's men, scattering over the entire working front, forced the lizard-collared men into the pits to unlock the diggers.

So furiously the rescue work proceeded, so intent were Doc's aids in effecting the release of every last one of the miserable fellows chained in the pits, that they were unaware for a time of a frightful trap closing in on them.

It was Monk who first became aware of their predicament.

"Blazes!" he roared. "There's lava on both sides of us!"

It was true. The seething lava flood had swelled, curled out in a broad path on each side of the plateau, straddling it. The only escape from the plateau of the honeycomb pits was by the sea.

Renny cracked his huge fists together, helplessly.

"The sharks!" he gulped. "Brothers, we're really jammed!"

Even as he spoke, the lava rivulets seemed to grow—like a doughnut swelling in a cauldron of boiling fat; the red ropes, fed by a continuous fiery flow from the spewing volcano mouth, swelled and swelled, pressing inward, threatening to engulf the entire honeycombed plateau.

Chapter XVIII

THE MOUNTAIN MAKERS

When Doc Savage took the trail of the count and Pat, his gold-flecked eyes ferreted out minute clues: a bit of shoe-crunched volcanic glass, a bruised leaf, missing barbs from a form of jumping cactus which grew rankly in the lava crevices.

Mounting upward toward the smoke-belching crater, Doc came shortly across in the crushed volcanic glass indisputable evidence that the Count Ramadanoff had met brother Boris's party and joined forces with them.

Trails of the brothers Ramadanoff led up and up the squat cone of the smoking volcano, headed directly for the fiery crater.

The trail grew fresher. Doc was high on the stubby cone of the mountain when the lava burst from the crater in an especially violent eruption. Flowing down in a mountain-high waterfall of fire in broad channels to the left of Doc's position, the liquid rock, like the spawn of many glass furnaces dumped together, sprayed heat and light through the sooty air.

Then, above him, Doc glimpsed those he trailed. A yellowish pall of smoke smudged them from view; but the glimpse had been enough. The bronze man left the trail and lunged upward on a shortcut which would allow him to intercept his enemies.

It was hard going over old, lava-flow formation. The stuff was deceptive. Twice the ground gave way beneath Doc's plunging feet and precipitated him into head-high ruts. Needle-point lava showered down upon him.

The ground under his feet became hotter as he proceeded; noxious gases, oozing from fumaroles, made breathing a hazard. Nearing his quarry, Doc, to avoid being detected, half slid, half climbed into one of the fuming, cinder caves and groped his way across the bottom between smoking holes gleaming a raw red color and noisily horrible with the suck and gurgle of fluid rock below the cinder crust.

With lids slitted to prevent his eyeballs from being scorched, he waded through that whithering heat and climbed the opposite slope of the clinker pit, maneuvering for a position which would bring him out above his enemies.

Doc gained the position—and then lost everything in the moment which should have been his greatest triumph.

The air in the deep fumarole he had just traversed was impregnated with an insidious gas—carbon monoxide—colorless, odorless, making its presence felt only by its sudden sapping of a man's strength. Doc had been aware of the possibility of this gas in the smoky atmosphere. Making his painful way across the scoria, or metallic rock froth, he had breathed no more than was imperative.

But even this little was too much. He felt a giddiness settle upon him. His legs grew leaden. Taxing his reserve strength to the utmost, he reeled to the top of the pit and then plunged down, an avalanche of needle-pointed clinkers sliding in a brittle wash behind him.

With his eyes momentarily sealed shut from the stinging reek of volcanic gases, his reeling steps had carried him onto a bubble-glass surface which had crashed under his weight, plunging him down a tortuous slope almost on the heads of his enemies. He was half buried in the downsurge of the metallic rock.

Before he could extricate himself, Boris Ramadanoff's revolver muzzle was a burning coldness against the back of his neck.

THE count stood in front of Doc, his bearded head thrown back, ghoulish mirth issuing in loud gobblings from his mouth.

"Everything, it is perfect!" Ramadanoff roared. "Better even than we could have planned it. Is it not so, brother Boris?"

Boris Ramadanoff nodded emphatically.

Pat Savage, imprisoned between two of the lizard-collared slaves, stared speechlessly, her face taut.

The count pointed a tapering finger at her. Even in the tenseness of the moment, Doc noted that the emerald was missing from the man's hand.

"We have the girl," the count rasped. "And we have you. And your other friends are trapped on the plateau."

Doc looked at the count, spoke in a composed voice. "No lava flow will flood the plateau of the honeycomb pits."

The count's eyes glittered. "One thing you have not taken into consideration. Brother Boris and I have long been prepared for this eventuality." He pointed with spasmodic eagerness. "Do you see that volcano crater?"

Doc said nothing. No one could have seen the crater through the smoke.

"It is mined with nitro charges," the count growled. "That is why brother Boris and I have climbed this slope—to explode those charges. With a new vent blown out for the lava, the plain of the pits will be covered with molten lava."

Doc shook his head. "You would not blow those charges."

"And why not?" the count asked.

"It is dangerous business tampering with the normal flow of volcanic lava," the bronze man reminded.

"If it were not for the fact that brother Boris is going to pull the trigger on the revolver which he is holding against your neck, you would see us dare it," the count said, ominously.

Doc, ignoring the threat, said: "There is still another reason why you would not flood the plain. That Devil's Honeycomb for which you have so long looked, digging your pits—you would hardly care to have it buried under a hundred feet of lava."

"So!" the count purred, dangerously, "you have deduced where the Devil's Honeycomb lies."

"Since the bronze man knows so much," Boris sneered, "why not tell him the rest of it, brother? Perhaps, in the world to which my trigger finger will send him, he will meet the *real* Count Ramadanoff, whose interest in this bit of unrecorded history will be vast."

"Agreed, brother Boris," the madman answered. He fixed his gaze upon Doc. "Know, then, that I am not the real Count Ramadanoff. The real Count Ramadanoff came to this island to escape the horrors of the Russian revolution. His vessel was that tramp steamer, which you, my dear Savage, so kindly located for us to-day.

"Escaping the revolutionists, the original count brought with him to this island a hundred people, artisans and noblemen. Of that hundred people, brother Boris and myself alone remain alive to-day."

"THE thumb-hole death doubtless accounted for the others," Doc remarked.

"Some of them died by the thumb-hole death," the madman admitted, readily. "Others went by the way of the pits. But you interrupt my story. Among the articles which the count brought with him was—well, the Devil's Honeycomb, among other things. This he cunningly hid."

"Brother Boris and I bungled badly when we killed the original Count Ramadanoff. He died before we had wrested from him the secret of his hiding place. Some things we knew, however. We knew that the Devil's Honeycomb is concealed on that plateau now encircled by red, running rock. So brother Boris and I caused ships to wreck, and, in that way, procured men to dig for us. The pits were dug to a system. It was our intention to honeycomb—the honeycomb part is humor, eh?—the whole plateau, if it was necessary——"

Doc Savage put in, "The tramp steamer? How did it happen that you failed to know its location?"

"It was wrecked in a tidal wave when the volcano erupted, and covered with volcanic ash," replied the other. "Neither Boris nor myself knew its location."

"But you knew about the compass, that it was the key to the whereabouts of the Devil's Honeycomb," Doc said.

Boris Ramadanoff started violently, peered at his brother. "You found the key?"

"No," the brother lied, quite calmly. "This man Savage is prevaricating, trying to turn your hand against me for his own gain."

"He knew the nature of the key," Boris snarled. "How did he know it was a compass, if he did not see it when you found it?"

"I tell you it's all a lie, brother!" barked the other, somewhat desperately. "Pull the trigger that will send a bullet crashing through his brain. We will end this!"

Boris scowled. "I would hear more about this compass key."

"Fool!" the bogus count hissed.

Promptly following the hateful exclamation in the smoky haze, there was a sound which might have been made by fingers snapping very hard. Boris slumped ominously to the ground, scarlet commencing to ooze through a depressed fracture in his temple. The "thumb-hole death" had struck again.

As a safety-first move, Doc Savage went into action. All during the bogus count's revelations, Doc had been surreptitiously working his knees and hips against the volcanic slag which had avalanched down and half submerged him, holding him to a degree. He had succeeded in loosening appreciably the hold of the stuff.

Now he lunged forward. Clinkers washed in a wave as his body heaved free.

He felt something close to his temple. The exact nature of it was hard to define. It must have shaved him very close, for his temple seemed to burn. It must have been the "thumb-hole death."

The bogus count suddenly lost his nerve. He lunged backward, spun around and started running.

Doc Savage shouted at Pat in the Mayan tongue. She twisted, lunged frantically; only her wrists were bound. So stunned were her captors at what had just occurred, that she managed to get free. Lunging, Doc Savage reached her side. Together they went over the edge of one of the smoke-ringed clinker pits. They ran furiously. Doc helped Pat.

Up to the right somewhere, hidden by the smoke, Doc Savage could hear the bogus count scrambling through the metallic clinkers. Judging from the strenuous sound, the fellow's main thought was to get away from the vicinity, immediately. His nerve had cracked, finally.

Chapter XIX

HONEYCOMB OF THE DEVIL

Pat demanded grimly, "Shall we follow the count?"

"We will," Doc Savage agreed; "but do not get too close to him. Make sure he hears us."

This combination of suggested action seemed to puzzle Pat. To remain behind the count and follow him furtively, she could have understood, but to follow him at a distance, and still let the man know they were doing so—that bewildered her.

"What's the idea?" she demanded.

Instead of answering her, Doc Savage paused and dislodged a heavy rock, letting it roll down a declivity. The man ahead had been traveling fast, but now he cursed. His speed became that of a madman. He knew they were behind him.

The earth had cracked in spots, probably under the force of expanding gases. They passed a stream of lava which had been diverted somewhere above and was already beginning to solidify in irregular waves, some of these head-high. In other spots, rivulets of the superheated stone twisted sinuously along.

They came to a region where imprisoned gases had long ago hollowed out the volcanic structure to form fantastic underground pits. It was as if monsters had dug dens in the sloping side of the cone. They waded through ground-glass-like clinkers in which they sank to the knees.

"It cuts like razor blades," Pat groaned. "My boots won't stand much more of this."

Unexpectedly, they came out on a level area, beyond which there was a sharp slope down to a cove. The wind was in their faces and it swept the dust back to the other side of the island. Accordingly, they could see a little better. Doc's flake-gold eyes scrutinized the terrain intently.

"Follow me," he directed Pat, and was suddenly gone.

Pat tagged after him as best she could. She was about exhausted. It seemed days since she had eaten, slept, had a peaceful moment, or drawn a breath of air that was fit to breathe.

A shout came from ahead; shots. She heard the count scream. Then Pat came on the scene.

It was at the edge of the little cove; the water was comparatively calm. Doc Savage was standing on the cove's edge, sheltered by a high boulder.

Fully two hundred yards away, the count was retreating warily along the beach, revolver in hand. He shot at Pat. She got undercover, crawled forward and joined Doc.

She looked at the bay.

A seaplane floated there—a high-winged, twin-motored amphibian, each motor being equipped with a three-bladed propeller. This ship was moored close to the shore, and on its fuselage a painted legend could be read:

COCOS ISLAND TREASURE
HUNTERS, INC.

"You headed the count away from the plane!" Pat gasped, suddenly understanding why Doc wanted their quarry to know he was being followed. It had kept the fellow frightened, had made him flee toward the plane. And it had worked.

"Right." Doc Savage waved at the plane. "That explains how the other brother got here. The must have been a treasure-hunting expedition on Cocos Island. There usually is, as a matter of fact. This plane was probably stolen from them."

This theory, upon later investigation, proved to be true. They waded out to the plane and climbed aboard.

THE big plane had a stout fuselage, one made for heavy work, which was fortunate, because the landing on the other side of the island, although Doc Savage made it expertly, was not easy on the hull. No plane could land easily in that chopping riptide.

Monk, Ham and the others, howling their delight, met the ship on the beach, wading out and seizing the hull to keep it from being damaged on the rocky shore.

"We can't clear outta here too soon for me!" Monk yelled.

"I gotta find Habeas Corpus. He's somewhere on the other side of the island."

"Probably with that herd of wild hogs still after him," Ham offered.

Doc Savage issued abrupt directions. "Monk, the rest of you, use this plane to ferry these poor prisoners of the count's to safety. Better take them out to the reef, not to the island. The reefs are not submerged, even at high tide. They would be safe there."

"What about you, Doc?" Monk demanded.

"The Devil's Honeycomb is here on this plateau," Doc Savage advised.

Pat had been thinking, apparently. Now, she said sharply, "Doc! That compass! There must have been a map in it, or something!"

"Undoubtedly," Doc Savage assured her.

"But the count took it away from me!" Pat gasped. "We haven't got it."

For answer, the bronze man brought from within his clothing the jeweled compass.

"It left the count's person when he took part in the struggle attending my capture. I picked his pocket."

Pat elected to stay. So did Renny. The others, being armed, felt able to take care of the prisoners, carrying them to one of the reefs near where the fake channel lights had decoyed ships to disaster.

There was light about them now; burning jungle ignited by lava, and lurid flashes from the cone took care of that. Doc Savage worked at the compass, got the glass out, lifted the card off its jeweled bearing. Beneath, tied to the bearing pin with silken cord, was a bit of parchment. Doc unwrapped this.

It was a simple chart, showing landmarks and paced distances.

They were lucky. The principal landmark, it developed, was a boulder of extraordinary size which reposed near one end of the plateau. They ran to this, pausing only to gather digging implements from some of the honeycomb pits. Doc Savage paced off the distances.

They began to dig—Doc Savage and Renny in the hole, Pat keeping the slag tossed back. They hit the leaden lid of a small chest some six feet down. Prying the chest out, they could tell that there were many other similar chests below.

"Let's have a look at the inside," Renny rumbled, and struck with his shovel. The lead was soft; it split. Huge globules of green and red glittered before their sweat-smarted eyes.

"Holy cow!" Renny breathed.

The contents of the lead box was an affair of gold, probably a part of an ancient breastplate of armor. In this were set the jewels. The design of the mounting was orderly and laid out in such a fashion that it somewhat resembled a honeycomb.

There were diamonds, rubies, emeralds, every one a stone that looked valuable.

"I can see why they called it the Devil's Honeycomb," Renny boomed.

"What about getting the rest out?" Pat demanded.

They began to dig for the additional chests. The sides of the hole promptly caved in, delaying them somewhat. A moment later, there was another misfortune, which entirely overshadowed this minor one.

There came a crashing detonation. The very earth itself seemed to convulse, leap upward, then shake, as if trying to split itself wide open. A great thump, queerly hollow, followed that. It was such a sound as characterizes the detonation of an extremely powerful explosive.

Pat looked appalled. "The count's nitro charge!" she gasped.

THEY looked toward the high volcanic cone, saw a sight which was probably the most spectacular, and at the same time the most menacing, they had ever witnessed. A rumble had started and was growing and growing. But that was almost unnoticed. It was the thing happening to the top of the cone that held their eyes. Niagara Falls seemed to have become molten fire, and was flowing upside down out of the great cone.

"Holy cow!" Renny rumbled. "That's what I call a Fourth of July celebration!"

Doc Savage straightened, glanced about rapidly; he was calculating the size of the eruption and appraising their distance from the beach.

"Run for it!" the bronze man said, abruptly.

Renny protested, "But these lead boxes——"

"Nothing like that is worth dying for," Doc Savage said, grimly. "If you stay to dig them out, you will not have a chance to get away."

Renny did not have to think it over long.

"You're right!" he thumped.

They ran for it, Renny pausing only to scoop up the cluster of mounted jewels which so strangely resembled a honeycomb—a honeycomb the cells capped, not with wax, but with scintillating brilliance.

The plane picked them up without much more difficulty than they had expected. They got away none too soon. As the ship lifted from the water and circled toward the more peaceful end of the island, they studied the scene.

Under a sky hell-red to the far horizon, the cone was spitting lava, boulders, some of the latter as huge as small buildings. A few of these great chunks fell into the sea, or rolled there, and sent up unbelievable quantities of billowing steam.

With the roar in their ears of a world coming to an end, and the light of an inferno before their eyes, Doc himself took the controls of the plane and landed it on the comparatively calm water inside the little cove. They did not beach the ship, but kept it off, with the motors running, ready for a quick take-off should an earthquake start. The latter was a possibility.

Monk, ignoring all arguments, went ashore. He wanted his hog, Habeas. Strangely enough, the dapper Ham—not at all dapper now—accompanied the homely chemist.

They were back unexpectedly soon, running, and they had Habeas Corpus.

"We found the other brother—the count—the one who was alive!" Monk yelled. "What do you think happened to him?"

No one made a guess.

"Those wild hogs!" Ham said, grimly. "They had finished with him by the time we got there!"

HABEAS CORPUS, Monk's pet, never a sartorially inclined porker at the best, now looked very bedraggled. That he had spent a hectic time on the fantastic island, was evident. He took every opportunity to lie down. He had been thin before, as thin as it had seemed possible for a porcine specimen to get, but now he was even thinner.

Renny jumped suddenly, squawled and grabbed his side. He looked somewhat foolish, examined a small spot which rapidly grew livid.

"What did that?" he roared.

Monk made a quick movement with his wrist, and something thudded against Renny's ribs again.

"Hey!" Renny said, startled. "What is that thing?"

Monk glanced at Doc Savage. "Had you decided what that darn thing was, Doc?"

The bronze man nodded. "The brothers must have spent much time practicing, to acquire such proficiency."

"Yeah, they sure must of," Monk agreed.

"Holy cow!" Renny grunted, examining the object which Monk held. "It's that big emerald ring the count wore! It's tied to a tiny thread, but you can't hardly see it!"

"And the thread is stronger than blazes," Monk told him. "You see, this is the thumb-hole death."

"But it seemed so mysterious," Pat said. "So sinister."

"It was both," Doc Savage interposed. "If you recall, the thumb-hole death struck only when the light was not strong enough to reveal the almost colorless cord. They threw the ring with great force. Both brothers were well muscled, you will recall. They must have practiced a great deal. Then they jerked the ring back with the cord."

"We found it on the count," Monk announced. "The wild hogs—well, they left it."

THEY fell silent after that, watching the scene before them. The rumble and roar of it. The leap and flash of gory light. The rumble of descending boulders. It was a fabulous spectacle.

Still, watching the volcano, they knew they were free to depart in the plane at any time and ferry the late prisoners of the brothers Ramadanoff to other and larger islands in the Galapagos, where sailors could call for them, as they later did.

Monk was exhibiting the honeycombed, jeweled breastplate.

"Not much, compared to what we probably left behind," he said. "But my guess is it'll sell for a million, anyway. Divided up among the prisoners we rescued, that oughta help a little."

If Ham heard that, he showed no interest. Ham had plenty of money, anyway. He was eying the pig, Habeas Corpus.

Ham suddenly emitted several loud grunts. He shuffled his feet noisily.

"Wild hogs!" he yelled.

Habeas Corpus never looked back. He hit the water swimming, and made for the safety of the plane.

"Boy, oh boy!" Ham grinned. "For years, I have been trying to find a way to make that hog keep out of my sight!"

THE END

To the world at large, Doc Savage is a strange, mysterious figure of glistening bronze skin and golden eyes. To his fans he is the greatest adventure hero of all time, whose fantastic exploits are unequaled for hair-raising thrills, breathtaking escapes, blood-curdling excitement!

☐	THE EVIL GNOME	2134	$1.25
☐	THE MAN OF BRONZE	6352	$1.25
☐	THE STONE MAN	6419	$1.25
☐	THE THOUSAND HEADED MAN	6471	$1.25
☐	THE RED TERRORS	6486	$1.25
☐	DOC SAVAGE: HIS APOCALYPTIC LIFE	8834	$1.25
☐	THE PHANTOM CITY	10119	$1.25
☐	THE MYSTIC MULLAH	10120	$1.25
☐	FEAR CAY	10121	$1.25
☐	LAND OF ALWAYS NIGHT	10122	$1.25
☐	FANTASTIC ISLAND	10125	$1.25
☐	QUEST OF QUI	10126	$1.25

Buy them at your local bookstore or use this handy coupon for ordering:

Bantam Book Catalog

It lists over a thousand money-saving best-sellers originally priced from $3.75 to $15.00 —bestsellers that are yours now for as little as 60¢ to $2.95!

The catalog gives you a great opportunity to build your own private library at huge savings!

So don't delay any longer—send us your name and address and 25¢ (to help defray postage and handling costs).